Andrea Bolter has always been fascinated by matters of the heart. In fact, she's the one her girlfriends turn to for advice with their love-lives. A city mouse, she lives in Los Angeles with her husband and daughter. She loves travel, rock 'n' roll, sitting in cafés and watching romantic comedies she's already seen a hundred times. Say hi at andreabolter.com.

Also by Andrea Bolter

Her New York Billionaire
Her Las Vegas Wedding
The Italian's Runaway Princess
The Prince's Cinderella
His Convenient New York Bride

Discover more at millsandboon.co.uk.

CAPTIVATED BY HER PARISIAN BILLIONAIRE

ANDREA BOLTER

MILLS & BOON

First Published in Great Britain 2020
by Mills & Boon, an imprint of HarperCollins*Publishers*
1 London Bridge Street, London, SE1 9GF

ISBN: 978-0-263-08759-8

MIX
Paper from
responsible sources
FSC° C007454

This book is produced from independently certified FSC™ paper
to ensure responsible forest management.
For more information visit www.harpercollins.co.uk/green.

Printed and bound in Great Britain
by CPI Group (UK) Ltd, Croydon, CR0 4YY

For Megan

CHAPTER ONE

THE EIFFEL TOWER. It had been a long time since Jules had woken up to the sight of one of the world's most famous landmarks. When his eyes clicked open after the heavy slumber he hoped would cancel out his jet lag, he'd used the remote control on the nightstand to raise the blackout blinds and let in the light of the Paris morning. There the tower stood in view through his window, in all its wrought iron lattice glory.

Jules's apartment was an example of the many Durand Properties, his billion-euro real-estate empire, he owned in the city with their mixture of historic architecture and every modern convenience. High ceilings, crown moldings and original chevron wood floors reminded him that this apartment in the Seventh Arrondissement, as Paris's districts were referred to, was over a hundred years old.

His eyes fell shut again. While there was no question that his hometown was one of the most magnificent cities in the world, he was uneasy returning to Paris. Traveling across the globe, buying more and more properties everywhere he went had become his way of life. The last sleep he'd had on land was on the fifty-seventh floor of an ultra-luxury hotel in Singapore. Always on the move, Jules liked living in hotels, anonymous and temporary.

After rubbing his eyelids with the heels of his hands, he reopened them. There was the window again with its spectacular view. The tower, watching over the city as it always did. Yep, he really was back in Paris.

Mindlessly scratching his bare chest, he knew he should get out of bed. Tomorrow, he'd resume his habit of starting the day with an outdoor run. Today, he'd acclimate. A busy morning lay ahead with reestablishing himself at the Durand Properties headquarters and completing the job he'd returned to France to do. It was time to take the reins from his irresponsible mother and father, who had been on their own globe-trot for far too long. Although parenting his parents was hardly how he'd envisioned this chapter of his life, blood was blood and he'd do anything he had to.

As if reading his mind, the buzz of Jules's phone beckoned and one glance at the screen's caller identification let him know it was his mother. He swiped to answer.

"Where in the world is my tall handsome son?" Agathe Durand's singsong led him to believe she was calling from a different time zone, as she was never chipper in the mornings. Her voice was high with that continental-traveler tone she used to fool people, to disguise the fact that she was perpetually discontent with her life.

"My apartment, Mother. You're not in Paris?"

"Tel Aviv."

"Tel Aviv. Dandy." Spending Jules's money, of course. "Dare I ask, is Father okay?"

"Yes, your exasperating pater is fine, although keeping me from properly enjoying Tel Aviv. The man wants to sit in cafés eating falafel all day instead of being out and taking in the sights."

There she goes again, Jules thought. Blaming his father for her own unhappiness. As she did the entirety of Jules's childhood. At their age, Jules hoped their domestic dramas were behind them, especially now that Hugo was confined to a wheelchair after a fall had broken his back. Yet, with his parents, there was no telling. The unpredictability of which drove ordered-and-organized Jules crazy.

"Never mind touring Tel Aviv. You're supposed to be in Paris. That's why I'm here." Arranging to meet them in the same place was often a challenge and Jules had sat waiting in many a foreign train station or airport, eventually receiving the call that they'd missed their departure.

While his parents continued their decade-long knack of finding an antique piece of jewelry to buy and then sell at a high markup, or one of them getting work in some corner of the world at a tavern or on a farm, Jules had been largely footing their bills. Hugo's physical condition now prohibited him from any hard labor. Agathe's bon vivant facade was not what it used to be and she was no longer able to charm her way into dinner or a night's lodgings.

As their only child, Jules felt a responsibility to them despite the dysfunction he'd grown up in. Money was something he had plenty of to give. So while peace and satisfaction were apparently out of the question for his parents, at least he could make sure they didn't disappear somewhere into the abyss. Now their wanderings had become impractical and dangerous. He needed to ground them.

In short, the gig was up for these nomads Jules called parents. It was time they stayed in one place. Paris, where they'd raised Jules in a shoddy apartment on the outskirts of town, long lost to creditors, was where they were born and where they would die.

"Oh, Jules, we'll be there eventually."

A wince reminded him of similar phone calls from years gone by. Only it wasn't both of his parents calling during any hour of the day or night far from home. It was his mother who, at least a dozen times during Jules's childhood, would become bored or angry with her housewifely doldrums. So she'd pack a suitcase and disappear, abandoning Jules and his father. With theatrical vows that she needed to *see* the world and would never return, she'd only get as far as visiting relatives in other parts of France for a few days. Inevitably, she'd regain her senses or outstay her welcome, not having the wherewithal to get any farther. She'd return to her husband and son with promises that she'd never leave them again. Until she did.

In later years, she began dragging Hugo along with her, which gave her the courage to venture greater distances. A bitter and cold man who was never able to maintain steady employment, it made no difference to him where he laid his head at night.

But this move would be final. Once Jules got his parents back to Paris and into one of his apartments where they'd have a safe roof over their heads, he'd base himself here again and look after what their aging health would demand. As laughable as it was to use the term for people his parents' age, it was time for Agathe and Hugo to *grow up*. In the process, Jules would call Paris home again as well, which he had been resisting but knew was overdue.

"If you had seen the way your mother behaved with our taxi driver last night, you'd be as horrified as I was," the voice of Jules's father came through the speaker. Obviously, Hugo had gained custody of the phone in Tel Aviv and was reporting to Jules lest his wife consider herself blameless for their latest row. "She absolutely threw herself at him. The young man was gracious, of course, but even he was embarrassed."

"You're just jealous," Agathe called into the speaker. Why Jules's parents had to fight during a call to him was anyone's guess. There was plenty of other time left in the day for them to badger at each other and then let things subside like they always did, neither of them having the gumption to actually end their marriage. They were becoming more childish every time he spoke with them.

"While I can't think of anything I'd rather do than listen to the two of you argue over the phone, I need to finish the apartment I have for you and run my business. You were supposed to meet me in Paris to make some decisions about the renovation. I'll put you in one of my hotels while we finish the work. Get here." He ended the call, annoyed. Hopefully, he was making the right decision in forcing them back. He couldn't think of another solution.

After showering and donning his uniform of a Savile Row business suit, he found his daily breakfast of a green vegetable smoothie in the refrigerator, which he had instructed the housekeeper to prepare. He readied himself for his workday in what was to become his new routine. Durand Properties occupied an enormous building in Montparnasse. It had been months since he'd set foot in his actual office, the staff spending more time with him on telescreens than in person.

Jules maintained a crack management team to collaborate with him on operations, leaving him free to do what he did best. Seek out real estate to purchase and rehabilitate, resell or lease. He was good at his job, he reasoned, as he'd amassed over two hundred properties on four continents.

He stood at his bedroom window and peered down at the street traffic while he sipped his green drink. People hurried this way and that, many headed to the metro stations where they'd travel underground to their daily destinations.

His eyes fixed on a young couple. The woman had a short haircut and wore a striped dress, gesturing wildly with her hands as they walked. Jules couldn't hear her from his second-floor apartment, but from her facial expressions she seemed to be shouting at her companion. The man, bearded and in jeans, listened silently. At one point, he deftly kissed her on the cheek without causing either of them to lose their stride. From arguing to kissing, their familiarity with each other made Jules guess they were a couple that had been together for a long time. Did interactions with women always have to include commotion?

"Yes, Karim." He turned from the window and paced the wooden floor as he took a call from his personal assistant at the office, who Jules spoke with several times a day regardless of his own whereabouts.

"Jules, I've checked with Lanon in Project Development about acquiring an interior designer to do the apartment for your parents. She tells me that all of our designers are swamped and if we pull anyone away from their current project, we won't make our completion dates."

"I see." Jules contemplated his assistant's report. A few years ago, he had bought a large building in the Second Arrondissement with apartments that would be a good fit for his parents because he was able do the structural changes needed for wheelchair access. Which was not always possible in the stately old buildings of Paris. Plus, it was in a lively neighborhood with plenty of shops and public spaces nearby. His tenant there had moved out, although later than he had expected. So the unit still needed paint, furnishings and decor, and some further accommodations given his father's mobility restrictions.

"I'll be in the office shortly. Please check with Giang in Resources as to how we should go about finding a designer immediately."

Of course, it couldn't be just anyone. Since the designer was to work with Jules as a son of the inhabitants as well as an employer, it wasn't a typical project. He'd want to select this hire himself.

"I already have. He suggested we contact some of our high-end furniture suppliers, as a lot of designers come through their doors."

"Good, then. Kindly get that done."

After the call, Jules knotted his tie in the mirror. He squared himself in the eye. The two little permanent creases between his eyebrows always gave his face a serious demeanor.

This morning, there was also worry in his big brown orbs. Converting abandoned factories into housing for an entire village in India was one thing. But taking charge of his parents' affairs, staying in Paris to be with them in their elder years was going to be his biggest project yet. He was fundamentally as unsettled as they were.

For some reason, he thought of that pretty girl in the striped dress on the street yelling at her man.

Returning to the window, Jules saw the couple far down the block now, as tiny as dolls from his viewpoint. He shifted his gaze to the Eiffel Tower one more time.

Paris.

The City of Light.

Home.

Jules had never felt lonelier.

"I might have good news," Yasmine Jaziri told her roommate, Zoe Gaiman, as she sat down at the outside table of the café on Boulevard Saint-Michel, the longtime haven for young people and students in the city's Latin Quarter.

Zoe nursed her lemon soda as she allowed Yasmine to get settled in. When the waiter approached, Yasmine ordered a glass of red wine.

"Let's hear it." Zoe couldn't wait. She could use some good news no matter who or what it pertained to.

"My boss, Si, told us that Jules Durand is desperately looking for an interior designer."

"Jules Durand? As in Durand Properties?" Zoe bubbled. The real-estate development corporation, which owned dozens of buildings in Paris and many more throughout the world, was founded and led by a certain Jules Durand whom Zoe had read about in a magazine article. The fact that he was much younger than would be expected for someone so accomplished had made an impression on Zoe, and she'd remembered the name. Also, judging from the couple of photos accompanying the magazine story, Jules Durand was twenty-five kinds of good-looking.

"Apparently, he has an apartment he needs work on, and quickly," Yasmine continued.

"What, he asked Si if he knew anyone?"

"Yeah. Si mentioned it at the staff meeting this morning." Yasmine apprenticed for Si Wu, a renowned furniture designer. Trendy and finely crafted side tables that cost more than Zoe earned in a year kind of thing. It made sense that Jules Durand would buy from a studio like that. "I can get you the contact information."

"I doubt he'd consider me qualified." While Zoe was a burgeoning interior designer, Durand Properties was not going to be interested in someone with her level of experience. She'd been in Paris for a year and had only managed to secure a few small jobs. A tiny restaurant that needed a new look on a budget. A nursery school that was updating their two classrooms. The couple that needed to utilize their parking garage for storage. Not much more than what she had been doing in Maupont, the small town near Lyon where she grew up. She had fled to make a name for herself in Paris, not to mention leave painful memories behind.

"What can I get for you two mademoiselles?" the older mustached waiter asked when he returned with Yasmine's wine.

"Thank you, we're just having drinks," Zoe quickly answered. There was no money in her budget for an expensive dinner. She and Yasmine had agreed they'd meet to savor a slow drink and watch the parade of Paris go by. At this point, even that was a treat.

The waiter snarled, no doubt hoping they were going to order food. Zoe shrugged her shoulders at him with a cute smile. It failed to crack his gruff exterior.

"It doesn't hurt to try," Yasmine continued on about Durand Properties. "You have nothing to lose."

"You've got that right."

Zoe had come to Paris on a hope and a dream, and feared that neither were coming to pass. Even sharing a one-bedroom apartment with Yasmine, whom she'd met through a mutual acquaintance, she couldn't afford this expensive city. Something had to give or she'd soon be letting her brothers in Maupont know that she was coming home, defeated.

"Just send an email," Yasmine encouraged. "You have some nice photos from the jobs you've done. Include those. You know what you're doing."

Sweet Yasmine. Always a word of encouragement. She assessed her roommate sipping from her wineglass Her thick dark hair was stick straight, as opposed to Zoe's corkscrew red curls that grew every which way out of her head. Yasmine hailed from Tunisia and had moved to Paris to study, eventually landing under Si Wu's tutelage. Even though Zoe's fantasy of success and a life in Paris seemed to be crumbling, she'd always wish the best for Yasmine.

"I suppose it wouldn't hurt to try and see if I can get a meeting." Not with Jules Durand himself, she hoped. That would be too nerve-racking. He'd probably have an underling interview prospective designers, wouldn't he? The CEO would have much more supervisory tasks in front of him.

What was she even thinking? Jules Durand's company, with some of the most notable buildings in Paris, was not going to hire someone who knew how to make a room look larger by placing mirrors in the correct locations! They would employ designers with CVs as grand as the rooms they'd be filling.

The waiter returned with a tray full of delicious-smelling food for another table. Zoe's nose followed the aroma as far as it could.

"Yasmine, you know what? You're right. I do know what I'm doing. I don't doubt my abilities." She liked saying those words out loud. "Durand Properties might be just the break I need."

"That's the spirit."

The possibility that if she did pursue the opportunity she might encounter Jules Durand himself niggled at her. Staring back at her from those magazine photos with his eyes as dark a brown as hers were as light a blue, he was one intense man. His were the kind of eyes that could take over a girl's thoughts. Make her wonder if the impossible might be possible. Not Zoe, of course. None of that was for her. But it might set someone else to speculation.

"Okay, get me the contact information."

Two days later, Zoe and her portfolio strode toward the Durand Properties headquarters. In her one good black suit with the coordinating silky blouse underneath, she felt professional and terrified at the same time.

Just as Yasmine had promised, the contact person at Durand Properties was easily reachable by email. He, in turn, sent her an e-log from which to choose an appointment time. Several of the slots were already filled, leading Zoe to deduce that other people were being interviewed, as well. Which didn't bode well in her favor as her competition might have more experience than she did.

Nonetheless, she was excited. This was why she came to Paris, to work within the walls of the incredible architectural marvels, both old and new, that graced this remarkable city. She loved it here, where the boulevards teemed with energy. She didn't want to return to sleepy Maupont, where the most she could hope for was the odd job revamping a guest bedroom or small office. Where, walking down every street, she'd see someone she knew who would give her that look of sympathy and pity for what would define her family's name there for the rest of eternity. No, Paris wiped the slate. Gave her a fresh start. And it was where she wanted to live for the rest of her life.

As Zoe neared Durand Properties, a modern glass building that occupied an entire square block, she ducked into an alleyway. Removing the comfortable shoes she'd been walking in, she opened her bag and extracted the business heels that pulled her outfit together. After the switch, she approached the entrance door, *Durand Properties* etched into the glass with a distinct script. An intercom system allowed her to announce her arrival, then the latch clicked and she was able to open the door.

She remembered that Karim Harbi, the man she spoke with on the phone, had told her to check in at the welcome desk before taking the elevator to the fourth floor. The woman who sat behind the counter verified the appointment and pointed her in the right direction.

When the elevator door opened to the fourth floor, Zoe stepped into a central reception area, the likes of which she had never seen before. People bustled to and fro. All the walls were made of glass, affording panoramic views of the city from every direction. The fourth being the top floor allowed Zoe to see that the slanted roof was made of a reflective type of glass and solar panels that could harness the sun's heat.

In the center of the space was a wide staircase with open steps and gray steel railing. Two women descended while engaged in conversation. Off to one side, a long concrete reception desk was staffed by three employees, two women and one man, all stylishly dressed in neutral colors, speaking into headsets. Several seating areas were grouped throughout with blond wood furniture, some with red upholstery, others bare. A cluster of men in suits sat at one talking amongst themselves. Low coffee tables held massive arrangements of red flowers. Abstract stone fountains placed here and there compensated for the lack of artwork given that there were no actual walls other than the glass perimeter. It was, quite simply, the most stunning workspace Zoe had ever encountered.

"Mademoiselle Gaiman?" a young man greeted her as she was taking in the surroundings. His voice served as a good reminder to make sure her jaw wasn't hanging open at the impressiveness of it all. "I am Karim."

His accent and dark skin suggested he was another young person who had come from somewhere else to Paris with a dream in his pocket.

"Nice to meet you."

"If you'll follow me, Monsieur Durand is ready for you."

What did he just say? As it was Karim she had been interacting with so far, Zoe had convinced herself that she'd be having her interview with him. Or with someone in their human resources department. Or someone other than Jules Durand himself.

"Karim," she coughed out, "is it typical that Jules Durand is the first to meet with perspective employees?"

"No, of course, a company of our size has a department devoted to personnel. But this is a special project of a personal nature. Jules will better explain when you meet with him."

Heart suddenly thumping against her chest, Zoe cleared her throat. Karim led her to a massive corner office, private by being delineated with its own glass walls. It was as carefully furnished as the reception area. As they approached, Zoe could see a meeting section with a wood table and chairs. There was also an area with two drafting tables, computer banks and shelves that held architectural blueprints. To the side of that, two white leather sofas faced each other with armchairs beside them creating a conversation space. There was a vase of more red flowers on a countertop beside a sink and refrigerator. A treadmill faced outward to the view. The single office in its entirety was large enough to house a family of four. At the stone desk in the center of it all, a man who Zoe recognized to be Jules Durand sat in a high-backed black office chair speaking to someone through an earpiece.

As she got closer, which for some reason felt like marching toward a firing squad, she could make out the furrows between his eyebrows that she'd taken notice of in those magazine photos of him. They gave him a sort of stern look that was somehow wildly sexy at the same time. In a dark gray suit, white dress shirt and forest green tie, he was as stunning as his office building. His aura, his buzz permeated the air and reached her all the way out in the corridor. This man was over six feet of pure power. Adrenaline pounded through her.

On impulse, Zoe began forking her fingers through her corkscrew curls in hopes that her hair didn't look too unkempt. She threw her shoulders back and stood as tall as she could which, given that she was a shorty, wasn't much.

Cheering herself on, she had this. She was a hard worker, had done nice designs in the past and deserved a chance to move onto bigger projects. Not to mention that the only way she was going to be able to stay in Paris was if she rose up to the next rung on the career ladder.

She was going to dazzle this man, regardless of how imposing he was.

He was going to hire her. No doubt about it.

Karim pulled open the heavy glass door to the private office and, after Zoe stepped in, took his leave.

"It's an honor to meet you, monsieur," Zoe began as she took an uneven step forward, which made one of her shoe heels wobble. Then she heard a cracking sound. But before she could do anything about it, the heel snapped and buckled under, jerking Zoe Gaiman forward and causing her to fall flat on her face into Jules Durand's office.

"Are you all right?" Jules dashed from behind his desk to attend to the interviewee who had just, literally, burst into his office. Presenting his arm for the young woman to use for balance as she stood up, he felt a surprising tingle when she wrapped her small fingers around his bicep.

"Yes, I'm fine," she quipped dismissively, although

nonetheless leveraging all of her weight onto his arm. The portfolio of photos and sketches she had brought along to impress him with was now scattered around her. A quick cheat of a glance told Jules that they were good.

Once she hoisted herself to a standing position, he took notice that she stood not much more than five feet tall. And she had a wild tangle of hair. Had her fall dislodged a more conservative hairdo? Because, at the moment, it looked like a crazed tree straight out of a Van Gogh painting. A wine-induced hallucination of reddish, no, almost orange spirals pointing toward every angle. It took all of his gentlemanly decorum not to reach out and touch one of her curls, so curious was he to know what they would feel like.

She retrieved the culprit that was responsible for her dramatic entrance. Indeed, the pointy heel had almost fully separated from the body of her shoe and dangled limply from its infrastructure.

"Darn it. These are my only..." She decided, flustered, not to finish the sentence. Instead, she slipped the broken shoe back onto her foot and used two hands to smooth down her skirt and jacket before extending her palm for a handshake. "I'm Zoe Gaiman. I hope you can forget what just happened and we can begin the interview over again." She blew a breath upward, possibly in an attempt to send some errant hairs back to their designated place.

As he returned her handshake, Jules couldn't consent to her terms because he had an inkling that he would never forget anything about Zoe Gaiman.

Her fingers were as soft as he'd imagined they'd be.

Together, the two of them bent down to gather up

the sheets of her portfolio. He gestured for her to take a seat opposite his at the desk. Hobbling on the broken shoe, Zoe made her way to the chair and slid in.

With a tap on his computer, a photo appeared on his screen, the secondary screen that faced Zoe's seat and on the large monitor that serviced the seating cluster to his right. In the past few years, Jules had conducted most of his work from his laptop while ensconced in suites of the world's finest hotels and in Durand Properties satellite offices. Naturally, he'd frequently returned to Paris for meetings and functions. But his highly efficient office here was underutilized. That was about to change, as he'd be basing himself here permanently.

"The apartment in need of design is in this building," he explained about the first photo to Zoe. Five years ago, he'd purchased the building, which had been divided into eight apartments, not knowing at the time that he'd be dedicating one to his parents. "Here are some photos."

To her credit, Zoe seemed to have recovered after her visit with his office floor and she studied the slideshow he presented. "There's an elevator, I take it?" she inquired.

"Yes. Which is critical. You see, this apartment is for my own parents to inhabit. My father is wheelchair-bound."

"Oh, so that's why Karim said this was a personal project. It looks as if the front entrance to the building has the width to accommodate a wheelchair, but the interior doorways have been widened? That must have been a tight squeeze."

"My architects supervised those modifications." Jules was impressed. Zoe was the third designer he'd interviewed today and neither of the other two had noted that obvious need for wheelchair clearance in the apartment's doorways.

He glanced away from the screen to make contact with her sky blue eyes, which had a crystalline shimmer he found very intriguing. She also had an adorable swath of freckles that ran from one cheekbone across her nose to the other. And that hair!

Women and their attractiveness or lack thereof was of no interest to Jules, so he surprised himself in even taking the time to observe Zoe's unique beauty.

"I see from your portfolio pages—" he pointed to what was now a haphazard stack that she'd lain on the spare chair beside her "—that you share my appreciation for blending the old with the new."

"Yes, I like to bring in every functional convenience but make the living space warm and stylish at the same time. And I did a course in special-needs accessibility. Let me show you some photos."

He peered over while she riffled through her pile. One looked like a guest room converted into an office, the other a classroom. Did she have the proper experience for an entire Paris apartment, especially one for his parents where he knew he'd demand perfection? Zoe showed him an unimpressive access ramp leading to a converted garage with a few grab bars installed here and there. Jules's contractors had already done the structural modifications on the apartment. Still, at least she said she'd studied accessibility.

He opened another program on his computer. "Here we have some suggested color combinations for the paint and furnishings in the main living spaces. We can look at the bathroom and kitchen afterward. I assume you're familiar with this software that automatically generates a primary color scheme with complementary shades for accents."

"I don't use auto-generated color combining."

"Excuse me?"

"I wouldn't want a computer to decide a paint shade to match a sofa color for me. That's not how I work."

With two fingers, she twisted a ringlet that fell over one of her ears. Jules had no way to determine if it was actually out of place. It was nothing short of ludicrous how curious he was about her hair. Although, now it was what was coming out of her mouth that alarmed him.

"Mademoiselle Gaiman, as you might imagine, Durand Properties employs every bit of technology available that can assist us in our work."

"With due respect, Monsieur Durand, computer-aided design is, of course, a marvelous advancement. And the furniture placement programs and whatnot on the market these days are timesaving tools. But I also have to feel a project. In my heart—" she paused to bring her fist to her chest for emphasis "—and in my soul."

"I see," he tittered, surprised at this young woman's pluck. People usually yessed Jules Durand, too intimidated to disagree. He wasn't sure whether or not he liked Zoe's assertiveness. Ever so briefly, his mind flashed on a very private way he might show her with his lips who was the boss.

He quickly refocused with, "I'm afraid I don't employ souls. I employ professionals who, in turn, follow industry standards and new developments."

"Does the way yellow spring flowers play against the five o'clock sky rely on a digital approval system?"

"I beg your pardon?"

"When the waves of the ocean ebb and flow, creating a natural rhythm that syncs with a shoreline wind. Can your computer software replicate that?"

Jules was becoming a bit irritated. While there was something mesmerizing about this young woman, he had a job to offer and expected it done his way, and certainly wasn't going to work with someone who questioned his methods.

Especially in dealing with this apartment for his parents, Jules wanted the project done quickly, as he expected Agathe and Hugo back in Paris soon and he couldn't accommodate time-consuming mistakes. He had no leeway for prima donna designers who constantly changed their minds and, for example, repainted several times before being satisfied with their choices.

He needed his parents securely ensconced, not traipsing all over the earth like vagabonds with his father in a wheelchair. It was ironic that Jules himself had called no place home for years, either, although his time away was well spent amassing a fortune.

Everyone was going to stay put in Paris. For all the turbulence of his upbringing, with his mother's abandonments and then returns, and his father's unstable employment history, Jules would ground them now. He'd become the de facto patriarch.

"I thank you for coming in, Mademoiselle Gaiman." He pushed his chair back from the desk, ready to show her to the door. "Obviously, we have an incompatible approach, but I do wish you well." Oddly, the idea of never seeing Zoe again gave him pause and he hesitated.

"Wait…" Zoe threw her palms up, trying to halt him before he stood. "If this apartment is for your own parents, don't you want it to breathe with life? Shouldn't it be a blanket of comfort? That sings in peaceful harmony. Why don't you show me the apartment in person? So I can feel it."

That was the second time she had mentioned *feeling* the apartment.

Jules didn't do feelings. He didn't choose properties based on spring flowers. He relied on engineers and architects and inspectors and financial advisors for whom the tools of the trade brought a scientific precision. Jules liked that. There was no room for gamble in his orbit.

Yet, chance was exactly what was in front of him. He'd get no data collection on how long his parents would live. There was no spreadsheet that could forecast if his mother would finally find serenity within the boundaries of a permanent residence. No analysis would report how good a job Jules would do as their caretaker.

So the last thing he needed was any further unpredictability. While he respected that Zoe was probably a very creative person, and thought he might contemplate for the rest of his life how hair grew out of someone's head like that, he had other prospects to meet with. This interview was over.

"Thank you for your time, Mademoiselle Gaiman."

He stood, hoping she'd follow suit. Which she did, but not before shooting a penetrating look at him that made his ribs rattle. Were there tears pooling in those bright blue eyes? "Good luck with the project," she muttered.

Jules saw Zoe Gaiman to the door with her tottering on her broken shoe heel all the way.

CHAPTER TWO

OBVIOUSLY WE HAVE an incompatible approach.

Jules Durand's words from the day before played over and over again in Zoe's head as she brought two cups of coffee to the teeny tiny balcony of her and Yasmine's apartment.

The window space with its wrought iron railing was barely big enough for two folding chairs and a stool they used as a table, but they loved to drink their morning coffee out there. It was special little things like that which made Zoe hopeful she could always call Paris home.

No matter that their balcony faced out to the rear of their building and overlooked the back of the building on the next street, which didn't afford a view of much of anything. They could still breath in the Paris air and see the way the sunrays cast this way or that, inspiring artists for centuries to capture that special light through their paintbrushes.

"You see the way the sun almost glistens off of the strawberry jam on your toast?" Zoe said to Yasmine as she handed her one of the mugs. "That's what I was trying to explain to Jules Durand. Everything is integrated in the world around us."

"Do you think that Jules Durand, of Durand Gazillion-Euro Properties, needed you to explain *anything* to him?" Yasmine asked before taking a sip of her coffee.

"Apparently not," Zoe snickered, as she maneuvered one of the chairs to the precise angle so that she could sit in it without falling over the railing.

"You haven't told me all of the details of your grand entrance."

"Yeah, I made quite a first impression. The only silver lining is that at least when I fell into his life, my suit skirt didn't hike up to show him my unmentionables."

"Glad you can see the bright side."

"Have I mentioned how much I hate high heels?"

"You say you like them because they make you look taller."

"It might not be worth it."

"So, did Durand give you a hard *no* or was it a *we'll let you know* kind of thing?"

"Oh, it was most definitely a *no*."

Thank you for your time, Mademoiselle Gaiman.

That was a hard *no* if Zoe had ever heard one. Especially with the kingly tone of voice he used and the way he stood up from his desk. Like he couldn't get her out of his office fast enough. She'd been so frustrated she almost ended up leaving in tears. Her shoe, his domineering demeanor, the rejection.

Although one thing not lost on her during their too short meeting was that if she'd thought Jules Durand was nice-looking in the photos she'd seen in a magazine, it was nothing compared to him in person. His thick black hair was cut short but left a little bit longer in front, accentuating the dense eyebrows with those crinkle lines between them. His eyes were deep and very dark, leading to a long narrow nose. With his closely shaven face and knife-blade jawline, Zoe had especially noticed his full lips, which were a pale pink. All united, it was one gorgeous face.

"Why are you smiling?" Yasmine interrupted Zoe's mental recap of the most handsome human she'd ever seen in her life.

"Am I?" She hadn't realized her musings were visible. "No reason."

"Tell." Yasmine chomped on her toast.

"Only that he was, you know, not too hard on the eyes."

"No kidding. I've seen pictures of him. He's tall and has a great build, too."

"He's the long and lean type. Not bulky."

Zoe thought of the impeccably cut suit he'd worn. And how regal he'd looked in it.

"He's always showing up on those eligible bachelor lists. And says he'll never marry, that the institution is not for him."

"He definitely has a way of letting you know he's in charge. Not very equitable."

Zoe looked to the sky. Maybe his arrogance was self-confidence, and that's what had brought him success. Or the other way around, that achievement had made him so sure of himself. In any case, there was more to him than that. A man who had given such detailed thought into setting up a workable home for his parents spoke to her. Maybe because she missed her own parents so much, his care and concern touched her heart regardless of his personal manner.

No matter, though. Zoe had no interest in the man other than professionally. In any man. Men could be distracting and lead to love. Love could lead to loss. She'd had enough of that already.

After she'd fallen into Jules's office, and her portfolio with examples of her work had scattered all over his expensive carpet, she hadn't had a chance to show him one job she had done for a wheelchair-accessible guesthouse in her hometown of Maupont. Maybe it wasn't on the same scale as the apartment he was redesigning in Paris, but if she'd have been able to show him photos of that project, might she have fared better in the interview?

What's done was done. Unless...? Could she call him and try to get another interview? No, that would seem like begging. She'd asked to see the apartment and he'd refused her. He was clearly uninterested in her style. As he said, they were incompatible.

"Do you have any other upcoming interviews?" Yasmine inquired.

"Not a one."

Zoe stretched her spine against the chair back. Still tired, her nights had been fitful lately as she tossed and turned, trying to figure out what to do next. She didn't want to retreat to Maupont, which was not the world's gleaming center of art and architecture where she'd dreamed of vital and fulfilling days and evenings.

Back home, her three older brothers ran the furniture shop that her parents had owned. Returning wouldn't be what she wanted, but they'd put a roof over her head and she'd help at the shop. Where sofas and headboards and lamps had ignited in her a fascination with indoor spaces that she longed to make a career of. And studied to do so.

Unfortunately, there was limited opportunity in

Maupont and its surrounding towns. Rarely was there new construction. Small business owners and residents lived modestly and seldom had money for large remodeling jobs. Or even needed interior design. Nothing there would ever give Zoe the chance to really spread her wings, to exercise her potential. She wanted big clients with big projects and big budgets. Paris budgets.

Plus, every road in her hamlet led to a sad memory. The town square where her parents took her and her brothers to play as children and afterward bought them an ice-cream cone. A small bistro where her parents would occasionally go out to dinner on a date night. How her mother would make that extra effort to put on a nice blouse and lipstick.

Or the train station. Zoe especially didn't want to have to regularly see the train station. When they were kids, her father would take them to watch the trains go by. They'd wave through the windows to the passengers, with Zoe always imagining the faraway places they might be going.

Sadly, the train station would instead come to represent the chilling reality that defined the Gaiman family. When Zoe and her brothers were young adults, their mother and father boarded their train to take the trip to Milan that they had been saving for. Little did the four siblings know that they'd never see their parents again. The train derailment that was the top story in all the local news killed their mother and father instantly.

Because almost no one ever moved to or from Maupont, all the townspeople there still looked at Zoe and her brothers with pity. It didn't seem to bother her brothers, or they didn't notice it as much as she did. The bent neck and mashed lips on people's faces that said

I feel sorry for you even if they were talking about the weather.

When her parents were still alive, Zoe had been reluctant to move away from them, even to chase her ambition. They were a close-knit family. Zoe got her university degree and worked on those small local jobs she acquired through shop customers that only served to make her thirst for the more complex ones. After her parents died, she and her brothers got on with things, selling their childhood home and taking over the shop. But eventually, Zoe knew that she either had to try to make her dreams come true or stop having them. There was nothing keeping her in Maupont. Her brothers supported her decision. And so to Paris she came. Now she feared her hopes had come to an end.

Snatching the last piece of toast from Yasmine's plate, Zoe nibbled on it.

Her phone rang. She glanced at its screen. The caller identification was blocked.

"Hello," she answered with curiosity.

"Zoe Gaiman?" The low voice was familiar. "This is Jules Durand. Would you be available to come see the apartment at one o'clock? I thought we might talk over the project again."

"Hello again, Mademoiselle Gaiman," Jules called out as he saw Zoe walking toward him. He'd arranged to meet her in front of the building where he'd soon house his parents.

"Monsieur Durand." She held out her hand for a shake. It was the second time he'd shaken her hand and couldn't avoid noting, as he had last time, its remarkable suppleness.

"Thank you for meeting with me."

"I have to say I was surprised that you called. I assumed you thought our interview fell flat," she said with a chuckle. "You know, *fell* flat?"

A tiny twitch raised the corners of Jules's mouth. "Yes, I know what you were referring to." He'd almost felt her embarrassment by osmosis when she tripped on that broken shoe and became intimately acquainted with his finely woven carpeting. No one would want to meet a prospective employer in that fashion.

"So, may I ask, monsieur, are you still considering me for the job?"

"I'll be honest with you. I was not impressed with anyone I interviewed."

"I see. I was the best of the worst in your estimation?"

"I didn't mean it that way."

"How did you mean it?"

"I...um..." Why was he befuddled around this young woman whose qualifications were less than he'd expect for this project that was of such personal importance? Something about her threw him off-kilter. Seeing her again made him realize just how much. It would probably be a very bad idea to work with someone as distracting as she seemed to be.

Nonetheless, she really was the best of the bunch that he'd interviewed. When he thought about the six applicants he'd met yesterday, Zoe did stand out. Plus, at least she had a bit of experience with accessibility needs. He thought he should meet with her again.

He watched as she turned her attention to the two wood doors painted navy with their bronze doorknockers adorned with depictions of a lion's head. The handles were original to the 1860 construction of the building. Of course, nowadays, a state-of-the-art coding system facilitated entry.

"I think it'd be a challenge for your father to get his wheelchair across this threshold." She pointed to the bottom of the door where there was a sliver of open space before it met raised concrete. "That wasn't visible in the photos yesterday."

"Yes." Jules liked that she was jumping right into the task at hand and had remembered that his father's needs were of primary concern. "My architectural team is working on some options. Let's go inside."

Jules punched an entrance code into the keypad and the door unlocked with a click. He pulled it open to allow Zoe in. As she breezed past him, sunshine caught that untamed jungle of curls atop her head. It was amazing the way the sun decided which spirals to highlight and which to let serve as contrast.

What was he talking about again? He had projects all over the globe, this apartment to finish while his parents were at present drifting the streets of Tel Aviv. He didn't have time to care about the sun's reflection on Zoe's hair.

If he were honest, it wasn't just his parents' whereabouts he had the most trepidation about. It was the prospect of spending so much time with them, of being face-to-face again with the tumult he'd been embroiled in his entire life. Despite Jules's demand that they return to Paris and *grow up*, as he sarcastically phrased it, he was going to have to keep an emotional distance. The commotion and neglect he'd experienced as a child had been kept at bay by his career and his world travels. Put to the test, those scars had only a very thin skin covering them.

Yet, this was something he had to do. The desperation in their voices during phone calls, the phony suave sophisticated pitch in his mother's tone signaled to him that their roving had to come to an end.

Once in the building's foyer with its marble floor, Jules tapped the button to call for the elevator, an old-fashioned cage style that had been added to the building in the early 1900s.

"Your parents will be able to maneuver this?" Zoe asked in reference to the accordion iron door that needed to be slid back in order to enter the not-so-large cabin of the elevator itself.

"The wheelchair will easily fit and there's room for another person or two to stand."

With no wheelchair inside at the moment, Jules was able to keep to one side of the cage with Zoe at the other as the elevator rose. Which was good, because he'd prefer not to stand beside her if he had the option—she might smell good. His eyes had already betrayed him with their inability to resist inspecting her hair in the sun. Now they were locked in battle with his brain that was instructing him not to look at her legs under that pink knee-length dress she was wearing. His mind lost the fight and his eyes pronounced the legs lovely and shapely. To which Jules almost frowned. Why did she have to be so attractive?

Once they reached their stop, Jules opened the cage and showed Zoe to one of the two apartments on the fourth floor. With another private code, he opened the front door.

"This doorway has enough width, and no threshold," she observed.

"Thank you. I'll let my architects know you concur," he said snidely, though she didn't react. He supposed she was trying to impress him.

The small entry area into the apartment led in one direction to the kitchen and the other to the dining and living room, which they stepped into. The floor-to-ceiling windows with double-glass doors that faced the street, as was typical in so many Paris apartments, would let in lots of fresh air. "Nice light," Zoe commented.

She looked behind her and then retraced her steps. Jules could tell she was imagining the entrance from the point of view of someone in a wheelchair.

"There are no hard turns from the front door to here," Jules confirmed.

"True. I'm thinking about a small shelf beside the front door at wheelchair height—" she gestured to the short wall in the entry area "—with some attractive bowls or baskets where your father could lay down his personal belongings or purchases when he came in. Maybe a painting or a mirror above it."

"Perhaps you'd like to make some notes," he suggested. "Did you bring a tablet or laptop?"

"I don't need to just yet. I'll remember."

"I expect every conversation we have to be documented."

"Yes, Monsieur Durand. I was just tossing out a thought."

"I'd like any ideas to be presented to me in writing or through images and cataloged with a filing scheme so that we might refer to it later."

"Every idea." Zoe gave him a side-eye as if she was

surprised by his request. Was she or was she not a professional? Her licensing and education seemed to be in order when Karim had researched her background.

Jules supposed she hadn't worked for a big corporation before and had a more casual relationship with clients who only needed a room redecorated and so on. It was frustrating that he couldn't find an applicant better suited to how he did business. He assumed that if he hired Zoe, she would want to do a good job and he could train her to use his methods. Although, as soon as he had that thought, it occurred to him that Zoe Gaiman didn't seem like someone who did things other people's way.

"I'm feeling Chopin in here," she said, making swirls with both wrists and outstretched fingers to animate. He noticed how tiny and fine-boned her hands were. "Soothing piano chords for soft hours after your parents have been out and about all day."

Case in point about methods. "May I ask, what does *feeling* Chopin mean with regard to the task? Neither of my parents play the piano."

"No, not literally. It's a mood."

"Is it?"

"Would you like me to write it down?"

He almost laughed. Was this young woman so opinionated with everyone she met, or just him?

The last thing Jules needed in his life was someone to argue with. He'd grown up in one long yelling match. He could remember crying in his bedroom as a little boy because his parents were so combative with each other. It was traumatic.

No, Jules worked conventionally and systematically and he expected all of his employees to do the same. If there was a dispute or disagreement, it was to be handled by one of his project managers. Although, in this case, he was to be the project manager as he would be directing the job given his personal interest in it.

Zoe must have sensed that he wasn't pleased with her little snip because she got that same glassy-eyed look as she'd had in his office when he dismissed her from the interview. Like she was about to cry.

Oh, women! Jules shook his head a little. One minute Zoe was bossy, the next emotional. After growing up in the mayhem of his parents, which was largely triggered by his mother's malcontent, he knew that he had a skewed view of women. He had wanted to believe that most women were not like his mother, full of acrimony and temper. Yet, he hadn't been able to prove his theory.

There'd been no one in his life he'd seen model a healthy relationship. When his parents weren't tearing each other down, they had a dull resignation toward one another. As if they both felt they were stuck in a trap, that there was no other choice. Neither had the guts to leave for good or put any effort into making things better. Agathe did her disappearing act but always returned. She donned a mask to the outside world and could masquerade as an extrovert, one who was apparently at present throwing herself at young taxi drivers in Tel Aviv. Hugo now had his wheelchair to hide in and blame.

Jules had no other relatives or people around him to set a positive example. And the women he'd subconsciously chosen during his university years and in his early twenties were dramatic and needy. It was what he knew. Once he gained success in his career, the opportunists began to descend on him, all sorts of women who would slowly reveal themselves to be only after what Jules could give them.

It seemed absolutely clear that women and Jules weren't a match.

He certainly had normal human desires. So, he developed a three-date rule. Which was serving him well. He could date a woman, but no more than three times lest he or she start to think any kind of connection was developing.

Jules was free to have the company of a female for dinner or drinks or recreation, even followed by physical intimacy should they both want it. He was allowed to repeat up to two additional dates with that same woman. After that, he cut things off, blaming his busy schedule if he liked her enough to explain why he wouldn't be calling again. His system worked like clockwork. He couldn't think of a single time he'd been tempted to break his rule. Zoe Gaiman's sassy and sexy mouth was of no concern to him in that regard. Coupling was not on Jules Durand's schedule.

"Do you think your parents will be doing a lot of entertaining?" Zoe asked Jules as they continued to survey the apartment.

Impress him with something, her brain screamed.

She'd already irritated him by commenting on something his architects were taking care of. Then she let out a little jibe about his rigid approach to work. That led to an awkward silence, which had been blowing like a breeze through the room for an uncomfortable number of minutes.

"I doubt it," Jules stated matter-of-factly. "Why do you ask?"

Hmm. Whenever Jules mentioned his parents, Zoe noticed a change of timbre in his voice. Like he was talking about people he didn't really know, other than that they were aging and his father was wheelchair-bound. Zoe wasn't sure what to make of that.

Don't voice your every thought like you always do, she counseled herself.

While Jules Durand was obviously a difficult man to deal with, Zoe needed to get this job. A reference from him could open doors for her. Her career could really take off if she got this right. The apartment was glorious—it had all the classic Parisian touches with the double-door windows and brass doorknobs. She would adore working on it, and others like it. Maybe she could *yes* him into thinking she agreed with everything he said and then do things her way after all. She'd do such a good job for him, he'd never notice. Although, clearly, Jules was not a man who missed anything.

"I was just wondering about what size the dining table should be, whether it would be frequently used for seating more than your parents. When *we* choose it—" she emphasized the word *we* as if she'd already gotten the job "—we could go with an oval or round shape for safety, no pointy corners. And we could order a couple of the chairs on casters so they'd be easy to roll out of the way if your father wanted to pull his wheelchair up to the table."

"That's worth a consideration."

"I'll make a note of it," she chipped, which earned her a funny double take from Jules, those creases between his eyebrows becoming very pronounced.

Standing next to Jules Durand, coupled with the afternoon sun creating a pleasant temperature, Zoe had a freeze-frame moment. If she got this project, her vision for herself could be coming to pass. By contrast, if she didn't, she'd have no choice but to return to Maupont, at least for a while. Maybe she could save up money and try Paris again in a couple of years. The mere thought of that brought a slump to her shoulders. She didn't want to return to her hometown with her tail between her legs, a failure, and nothing but harrowing memories to look forward to when she got back.

"Is something wrong?"

Zoe subtly dabbed the outer corner of each eye to wipe away the drops that those very thoughts had produced. "No, not at all, Monsieur Durand. This apartment just really speaks to me about the beauty of Paris."

A wistful smile crossed Jules's lips, the first one Zoe had seen. She almost keeled over, and this time it would have been *his* fault.

If Jules Durand was handsome with his serious professional face on, the way he looked while smiling was something from another dimension. Laugh lines defined his mouth, which opened enough to display perfectly straight white teeth. Yasmine had told her she'd seen his photo on those silly Paris's-Most-Eligible-Bachelors lists the gossip magazines did. It was not hard to see why, although she did wonder why this gorgeous and powerful man was still a bachelor.

Zoe didn't exactly know what caused him to grin, but she'd walk ten miles in the snow to be able to do it again. *Make Jules smile.* She'd add that to the list he wanted her to keep.

"I appreciate your enthusiasm," he said by way of explanation. "It is a marvelous property, without question."

They smiled at each other for a minute that Zoe

would swear had nothing to do with architecture. Thinking quickly to prolong the positive interaction she asked, "Can we have a look at the kitchen?"

"Please." He gestured for her to enter ahead of him.

He pulled his phone from his pocket.

Standing side by side, surveying the kitchen, Zoe became immediately aware of being in such close proximity to him. He produced an inner heat that she instantly liked and felt drawn to. With him being so much taller, she could have nestled her face against his shoulder and, strangely, thought about doing just that.

Instead, she had to not only discreetly turn her head, but also crane it upward to get a glance of his face in profile while he tapped into his phone. As he concentrated on what he was doing, his strength and potency was tangible. It made the skin prickle all over her body. She'd never been in the presence of someone who controlled the oxygen in a room.

Once she was able to pull her eyes away from him, she saw that the built-in kitchen cabinetry was complete, but doors were not affixed and there was no backsplash as yet.

"I'm thinking of this for the cabinet." He showed her what he'd cued up on his phone. French country wood with intricate arch carvings. She didn't like them. The apartment had enough ornate touches. She'd choose something simpler for the kitchen. But she didn't say anything. Yet.

The client was always right, so the saying went. That was until she could sneak in her own ideas and make clients think they had thought of them on their own.

Just get the job, she advised herself again.

A cream-colored granite countertop was in, which

delineated the kitchen from the front entry area. An idea came to mind that she couldn't resist pitching, even though it would mean redoing work that was finished. "Why don't we lower that granite counter and take the cabinets out from underneath?" Again using *we*. "There is plenty of other storage elsewhere and that would leave open space so that your father could just wheel right up under it. We'll make it a breakfast bar with a chair of the same height for your mother."

"Go on."

"I know it would require a change order and add some cost. But you don't have the cabinet doors yet so at least those won't be wasted."

Jules's heavy eyebrows hitched up.

So, Monsieur Durand was going to be surprised every time she had a good idea? That was fine with Zoe. She had lots of them.

"I can picture that. I'd like to see the specifications. In writing."

"Also, if we go with a style that's less fuss…" Zoe stopped herself again. She wasn't going to tell him that she didn't like the cabinet-door style he'd chosen. There was time for that later. He seemed to be responding favorably to the suggestions she was making for his father's special needs. She should stick with that for the time being. "I'd also like to shorten the length of the counter so that your parents have more room to pass through. And if the stone is cut properly, that extra piece of countertop can be salvaged to create the entry shelf I was talking about."

Jules looked at his watch that Zoe assessed clearly cost more than the salary she made last year. Was she losing his attention?

"I've got an appointment in ninety minutes. Followed by two more. I need to get some lunch."

"Oh," she stuttered after his abrupt change of topic. "I'd love to talk more about the project sometime."

"Yes. We'll have lunch and discuss it further. Was there something unclear about that?"

"Only that when you said you needed to get lunch, I thought you meant... Never mind, Monsieur Durand."

"Why don't you call me Jules?"

"And I'm Zoe."

"Yes. I know."

"I mean, call me Zoe."

"Your name."

Why were they back having so many miscommunications after they had just jived a few seconds ago about the countertop? She didn't understand the way he thought. Although she had the sense that she'd like to.

During the elevator ride down, Zoe observed everything she could about the building's structure. On the street, she followed Jules a few doors down to a bistro he knew. She was thrilled at the moment. Like something from a movie, she was in Paris with a dashing billionaire. It almost wasn't real. They took seats at one of the small tables outside in the fresh air. Everyone who walked by seemed so chic as they went about their business. French women really did knot their scarves a certain way and beard stubble on men never looked better.

When the waiter presented them with menus, Zoe had a moment's panic. She didn't want to assume that because Jules was wealthy he was going to buy her lunch, as he hadn't expressly said so. With her dwindling bank account, she'd need to mind what she ordered.

"Two glasses of the Domaine du Candulon Sauvignon Blanc," Jules ordered before the waiter left. Then asked her, "Is that all right?"

She didn't want to tell him that she'd had so little work she needed to conserve her money. A glass of wine couldn't cost that much, could it? Except that when she found on the menu which vintage he'd ordered, she was wrong.

"I'll take a garden salad with grilled chicken. Would you like the same?" he asked Zoe when the waiter returned. "I'll buy lunch, of course."

Zoe wondered if she was blushing. At how utterly mesmerizing that famous real-estate tycoon Jules Durand was telling her that he'd buy her lunch!

But she wasn't going to bat her eyelashes and let him choose what she'd eat. "No, thank you. I'll have the forest ham and creamed butter on a baguette."

"Really?"

"What do you mean?"

"I prefer a lunch of lean protein and vegetables. That nourishes me for the afternoon."

Another difference between them. Zoe ate anything that was put in front of her and had a special love for the baked goods of Paris.

It shouldn't surprise her that Jules was rigid about his lunch, just as he seemed to be with everything else. Zoe wondered what, if anything, made this man cut loose. Did he have a wild side? Something about the possibility of that rumbled low down in her belly.

She gobbled the first half of her sandwich when it arrived, causing Jules to smirk a bit.

"Were you starving?" he commented on her dedication to her lunch.

"It's just so delish. Do you want a bite?"

"I don't eat bread early in the day. The carbs slow me down."

She shrugged and took another humongous bite of her sandwich. There was no bread o'clock in her regime. "So I'm guessing you won't want to order dessert?"

Jules ate his salad with vigor while fielding messages on his phone. He shook his head. "I've got to take care of this right now. If you'll pardon me."

"Go ahead," she said, still chomping enthusiastically at her sandwich's salty richness. Should she be pretending she had urgent business to attend to on *her* phone, as well?

"Karim," he spoke into the phone, "set up a meeting for me with Kowalczyk. Today."

After issuing five different sets of instructions to Karim, Jules finally put down the phone and sipped his wine. He made an assessment of Zoe, as if he were sizing her up. "I have a full schedule, and a number of projects that have presented challenges in addition to moving my parents into the apartment. Therefore, I can't spend any more time interviewing for an interior designer. Zoe Gaiman, you have just gotten the job. Effective immediately."

CHAPTER THREE

JULES SIPPED HIS green breakfast drink while gazing out his office window at the morning sky. He and Karim had just finished their morning meeting, the newly in-person chat as opposed to the daily teleconferences they'd been having with Jules checking in from the four corners of the world. There was a lot on Jules's mind, with properties in various states of flux from Kyoto to Morocco to Perth that all needed his review. Yet, he found himself staring out into the distance, longing for something, not knowing what.

"Mother," Jules answered with a tap to his earpiece when his phone's buzz identified the caller. He girded himself before asking the inevitable. "Where are you?"

"Still in Tel Aviv, darling. We met a fabulous French couple last night. Two gentlemen who own inns up and down the Loire Valley. I spent the evening dancing with Gaspard and Louis, while your father sat and drank."

Jules pursed his lips. How like his mother to be critical of his father who, obviously, wasn't the type to be out on the dance floor in his wheelchair.

He could hear over the phone that Agathe was wearing her disguise again, like she was genuinely attacking every day with gusto. He could hear the reedy thinness in her voice, as if she were trying to convince herself as much as she was him.

"At your ages…"

"Oh, heavens, Jules," she cut him off, "you sound like an old fuddy-duddy. When was the last time *you* were out dancing all night?" Ah, so Agathe also had managed a dig at her son.

But with a shrug that no one saw, Jules tried to think of a time he'd stayed out dancing. Never. That was the answer. He did not spend his evenings carousing. Early to bed and early to rise was more his routine. He couldn't say it was fun, but it made sense for his life.

"To what purpose do I owe this delightful update?"

"We're a bit short on funds."

Jules scowled. Not really about the money, which he had plenty of. But his mother's frivolous attitude irked him. "This is the last time. There are plane tickets to Paris already purchased in your names. I've hired a designer for the apartment and unless you want to leave all the decisions to us, you'd better get here." That wasn't much of a threat to her and Jules knew it. She wouldn't care, might not even notice, what style of cabinet door was in the kitchen or the fabric of an armchair.

Agathe was no domestic maven. She always thought she married beneath her and said so at every opportunity, even though her family was of the same working class as Hugo's. They met while he was tending a bar at a local brasserie in the Paris suburb where they both lived. Agathe and some other girls from the neighborhood happened to wander in one night. When Agathe told the story in retrospect, she'd say she was attracted to what she called Hugo's *sad* eyes. The same eyes Jules inherited, according to his mother. Hugo and Agathe began to date and before long she found herself pregnant. Their wedding was held three months before Jules was born.

He remembered as a young boy that his mother spent her days on time-wasting activities like watching television and pouring her first glass of wine before lunchtime, never embracing motherhood or embarking on a career. And Hugo drifted from one job to another, ornery and short-tempered perhaps due to unresolved issues about his own relentlessly critical father.

Jules grew up in a household filled with mood swings that felt like arduous climbs up a steep mountain followed by sharp drops down, wherein the trek began again. And again and again. His parents' fighting might have begun over something as trivial as Hugo leaving his coat on a chair instead of hanging it up. Then the bickering would escalate over several days' time, culminating in his mother packing her olive green luggage and leaving, claiming she'd never return. Jules lost track of how many times it happened, but at least a dozen.

By his teenage years, he was no longer rattled by the abandonment he'd endured as a younger boy, when he'd stick his head out his bedroom window to watch his mother storm down the street away from their dingy apartment, yanking on the handle of the suitcase tottering behind her on its worn-out wheels.

Hugo barely looked up from his newspaper when she left or when she returned. Jules never found an ally in his father. The most Hugo would manage during his wife's absences was to bring home a few groceries at night and sign his son's school forms. There'd never been any commiseration with his father over his mother's behavior.

Jules had his first job by thirteen years old, sweeping the sidewalk for any shopkeeper who would pay him for the task. When he was twenty years old, during his university years, Jules had saved enough money to buy a ramshackle apartment in a downtrodden area. He cleaned it up, leased it and began to learn the ins and outs of being a property owner.

"Toda raba."

Agathe must have thought she was being cute by thanking Jules in Hebrew for agreeing to send money.

He ended the call and returned to scrutinizing the sky. It was a cloudy morning in Paris but the weather forecast predicted it clearing later in the day when he'd be meeting Zoe. The thought of seeing her again brought a smile to his face, which was welcome after he'd just been irritated by his mother. Zoe's orange curls. The petite willowy body that had zigzagged through the crowded boulevard yesterday with snakelike flexibility. The ideas for the apartment that she was so sure and confident about. She'd had some worthy suggestions. That she was full of enthusiasm peaked Jules's interest.

As unlikely and unexpected as it was, something about Zoe had gotten under his skin. He'd thought about her before he'd fallen asleep last night and again first thing when he woke up. He'd even checked his watch a couple of times already, eager for their afternoon appointment. Which was absurd. He kept people at a tidy distance aided by the fact that they were often intimidated by his wealth and position. He served nicely as his own barrier.

Daydreaming about seeing a woman again was not how Jules played the game.

By the time he'd finished having lunch with Zoe

yesterday, he had too much else on his mind to continue looking for a designer and decided to give her the project. Lest his new hire think she'd be given free rein on the apartment, Jules planned to show Zoe some of his other properties in Paris. To make clear what he liked. While he appreciated that she spoke up about her thoughts, he'd make sure that by the end of the day Zoe understood that all final decisions were to be his.

Despite his affirmations about who was in charge, when he saw Zoe coming up from the metro station later that afternoon, Jules felt a lurch in his gut. She was so pretty with her bare legs under a full floral skirt worn with a low-cut midnight blue top. As she got closer, he noticed the freckles that dotted her face were not the only ones on her body. Her collarbone and exposed décolleté were adorned with more of the pigmentation marks that he found oddly charming. For a minute, he found himself almost angry with her for being so lovely. Women didn't sidetrack him, and he was determined to keep it that way. What sorcery was this one carrying up her bright blue sleeve?

"Zoe."

"Jules."

He gestured to the building a few steps away. "Built in 1901. I want you to see an interior design we did in one of the apartments. The tenants are at work and have allowed us to let ourselves in."

She commented once they had entered, "No elevator?"

"No, in this particular building one hadn't been put in over the years, and we couldn't do the structural changes it would have required."

"So it's not suitable for elderly people."

"No, but we've never had any problems leasing it. The stairs are good exercise."

Zoe followed Jules up the steps and by the third floor she was huffing for breath.

"Would you mind slowing down a minute?"

Jules sneered to himself, his face not visible to Zoe behind him. He had indeed been bounding up the stairs. Was he trying to impress her with his physical prowess? So unlike him.

They entered the apartment. It was another well-preserved example of historic Paris interiors.

"Oh, so you went very traditional here?" Zoe commented at first glance.

"Yes, we chose the Tiffany lamps and the rug has details woven in Chinese silk."

"Do you lease all of your properties already furnished?"

"No, just as often they're empty. But here in Paris, our clients tend to be of a standing that utilize the full services we can offer. Expense is rarely a consideration."

"And they choose the design themes?"

"What are you implying?"

"Nothing." Her voice rose an octave. "You've got red walls, gold draperies, the large wood-framed sofas with embroidered cushions."

"I take it you don't like it?"

"Only that I gravitate to more comfortable styles. It's just my personal preference. Again, my opinion, but I think there's opportunity to highlight the period pieces without dominating the whole room in this sort of bordello style."

"Bordello! I'll have you know these fine antiques took a year to locate and cost ten times what it would have to simply recreate the pieces. We used university documentation for authenticity."

For as many times as he'd thought about Zoe in the past twenty-four hours, he seemed to have forgotten that while there was something extremely appealing about her, she was exasperating, as well. Jules did not surround himself with uninhibited people who voiced every thought they had. Squabbling was the last thing he wanted to do with employees, and saw to it that he never did.

Oh, no. His parents were evidence that life was too short to be spent arguing, even for the Zoes of the world who found discourse to be some type of sport. So, it was with a jaw tensed shut that he continued to glare at her, trying to remind himself that her personality didn't matter. As soon as the apartment for his parents was done, she'd be out of his world forever.

"No disrespect intended. I'm sure your tenants love their surroundings. I was just thinking out loud. Isn't an exchange of brainstorming exciting?" she asked in earnest. "You wouldn't have hired me if you wanted someone who would agree with you all of the time."

"And I expect you not to make me regret my decision."

Jules massaged the divots between his eyebrows and began the diaphragmatic breathing a podcaster had been explaining through his earbuds on his morning run earlier.

"Do you have brothers and sisters?" Zoe asked. Was she trying to change the subject?

"No. Why?"

"Only that I grew up battling with three older brothers. Let's just say that confrontation is something I'm quite used to."

So was Jules, but for all the wrong reasons.

Therein lay the difference. Zoe understood arguing as something organic and useful. Jules's parents fought in a way that belittled the other and had no end goal.

Zoe was right, though. Arguing over a bordello— *ha*—lamp did not mean anyone was leaving or being hurt. It was just heated conversation. Jules didn't know why Zoe pushed those buttons in him. Or perhaps it was the apprehension of spending more time with his parents, who hadn't evolved in their thirty-four years together but hadn't parted, either. In their own weird way, they were still very much a couple. Agathe no longer had it in her to leave Hugo's side. But fighting was simply their way, their cycle. Jules had long ago decided it wasn't going to be his. Hence, his three-date rule to be sure he didn't accidentally hope for a different outcome.

As they left the apartment, Zoe swept passed him and he got a whiff of what smelled like coconut shampoo. Without realizing it, his head bent toward the scent as if to follow it through the doorway. He quickly righted himself, shocked by his own actions. Zoe was making him *feel* things. Which was frustrating and baffling because Jules Durand had gotten as far as he had in life by shutting down feelings. At all cost. How high would the price get?

"I don't understand him at all," Zoe exclaimed to Yasmine as they sat cross-legged on their small sofa while watching a cooking show on television. "In one moment he's nice to talk to and then in the next he gets holier than thou."

She reached over for one of the strawberries in the

bowl on the coffee table in front of them. After several hours spent with Jules looking at a few of his luxury properties around town, they'd parted company. He offered to have his driver give her a ride home but she opted for the metro, knowing that she also wanted to pick up some food on the way. She and Yasmine nibbled on the berries, the chicken and loaf of bread she'd brought home. They'd eat the leftovers tomorrow.

The TV chef was shelling a lobster with her impressive knife skills.

"Well, he gave you the job, didn't he?"

"Theoretically. Although he makes me nervous that I could blow it just as easily with one wrong turn."

"Don't make one, then."

Yasmine was right. Zoe needed to keep tabs on her freewheeling style. There was no money left to keep hope churning if she lost this job.

The meeting had gotten off to a rocky start when she likened that first apartment to a house of ill repute. But it was so over the top she'd just blurted out her opinion. Censoring herself didn't come naturally.

"That's probably why he's at the top of his field," Yasmine continued. "By doing things his way."

"How he talks about design choices is driving me crazy. This color matches with that building material, which mathematically coordinates with a certain number of chairs. It all makes perfect sense but there's something so flat about all of his computer software and texture charts."

"At work, we have designers who come into the shop with specifications like that. They want a sofa in blue velvet shade number such and such, and bigger than x but smaller than y. Then just as many come in not certain what they're after but they know it when they see it."

"Right, so I'm the latter, he's the former."

"Just because you're not a high-tech planner like he is doesn't mean he won't be happy with the outcome."

Zoe broke off a piece of the country bread and stuffed it in her mouth. The center was chewy and moist with an airy crumb that made her mouth do a happy dance in response. The chef on TV tossed a large knob of butter into a sizzling skillet.

Zoe thought back to the lunch she'd had with Jules when he told her he didn't eat bread at certain times of the day. While she certainly didn't begrudge anyone healthy eating habits that worked for them, this was Paris! Where even the simplest bread was elevated to an art form. How could he resist the smells and tastes that beckoned to passersby from the storefronts at every turn?

Once again, it was systems and discipline that defined this man's life.

"He can be so annoying."

"Oh, so you're attracted to him! That explains everything."

"What?'

"He wouldn't peeve you if you weren't into him."

"I'm not *into* him." What a silly term that was! "I'm *into* keeping the job and staying in Paris."

"Okay, I'm just saying there's a twinkle in your eyes when you talk about him."

"There is not!"

"Suit yourself," Yasmine said and then wedged a too-big strawberry into her mouth. They both laughed.

On TV, the chef swirled the butter until it was brown and then gently eased the lobster pieces into the pan.

Even if she did find Jules alluring, an elegant billionaire like him wasn't going to be interested in the frizzy-haired little designer he half regretted hiring. For starters.

The second reason for any contemplation of Jules's appeal being ludicrous was that Zoe was never going to get involved with a man. She was never going to love. Nope. That was already decided. The edict signed and certified. Because if there was one thing Zoe had learned the hard way, it was that to love meant to accept the possibility of loss. And Zoe couldn't afford to lose anymore. As it was, the bits and pieces of her heart were barely being held together. She might be willing to take a risk on a paint color, but not with her love.

The phone call she would never forget replayed in her mind.

It hadn't been but an hour earlier when Zoe and her brothers had accompanied their parents to the train station to see them off for their long-planned trip to Milan. Zoe's mother had dressed nicely for travel, an expression of her excitement about the journey to a fashionable city.

Zoe would forever remember the burgundy-colored pantsuit with a patterned blouse underneath that her mother wore. Her long hair was held back with a pretty barrette. She had even convinced their father to sport his black leather jacket and dress jeans so that they looked like a smart couple on the go. Zoe and her brothers had presented their mother with a nosegay as a bon voyage.

At twenty-three, Zoe had long finished growing and

was clearly the short one of the family, taking after her maternal grandmother who had been barely five feet tall and had the same unique red hair. Her three brothers towered above her as they all gave hugs to their departing parents.

After getting on the train, her mother had made sure to blow kisses to her children as they pulled out of the station. They were to be gone for ten days. No one could have guessed that these four siblings waving on the platform would never see their parents again.

Afterward, back at the furniture store, Zoe retreated to the office to do some bookkeeping while her brothers manned the sales floor. When the phone next to her rang, she casually picked it up, assuming it was a potential customer inquiring about an item. Instead, the caller identified himself as a police officer, and from his subdued tone Zoe knew instantly that something was wrong.

Her ears listened but they could barely hear. With each word uttered, the voice on the other end of the line sounded farther and farther away.

Train derailment... Fifty-seven dead... No survivors... Sincerest condolences... Counselor to come by...

What followed was a blur of days upon days of neighbors bringing over soups and casseroles and cakes that had no taste. Coffee was no different than water, midnight was not distinguished from dawn. Relatives Zoe hardly knew descended from both within and outside of France, sharing their sets of remembrances. Psychologists and social workers spoke in the hushed and modulated pitches they no doubt received training for, designed to calm the listener but which struck Zoe as forced and artificial. The questions never ceased about what was going to happen next, to Zoe and her brothers, to the store, to the house they'd grown up in.

There were the tears that wouldn't stop. Like a re-circulating fountain, for as many as erupted from Zoe's eyes, there were still more behind those waiting to spray forward. She'd hardly believed she could cry that much without dehydrating all the liquid in her body.

As the weeks went by, the visitors and stringy meat stews stopped arriving. The spring of tears eventually lost some of its force. It erupted every day, but the flow wasn't as strong and didn't last as long.

What replaced it was something small but heavy that sat on top of Zoe's rib cage and never moved from its spot. It reminded her that her small body couldn't house a second souvenir of bereavement like the one she carried. She'd never ask it to. Yet, the potential for loss was all around. When Zoe caught herself caring too much about anything, that little spot pinged and sent a subtle vibration through her body. A warning sign she relied on.

So whether or not she was fascinated, and pinged, by Jules Durand was a moot point. Obviously, a fling with her boss, and yes his attractiveness was indisput-able, would be a very bad move. And anything more serious was out of the question for her. Not to mention that she had no cause whatsoever to think that he was interested in her.

There was absolutely no reason to keep replaying the moment at that second property they'd visited today, the attic apartment with the steel-framed skylights. It was an innocent gesture of chivalry, the way he placed his hand on her lower back to usher her through a doorway. That it sent a wicked shiver up her spine, snapping her shoulders to arch sharply, didn't mean anything at all. Nothing at all.

It simply wasn't important that she still had the sensation of his large hand on that exact spot, imprinted like a tattoo. When he'd whispered, *Come this way*, he'd meant nothing by it other than to guide her into the room. But his low voice had been so close to her ear it reverberated for the rest of their time together.

Why was she still thinking about that interlude?

Come this way.

Dish completed, the TV chef placed the pieces of lobster onto a serving plate and drizzled the brown butter on top. She then sprinkled on toasted breadcrumbs and chopped parsley, declaring that the most important ingredient in any recipe was quality.

"*What* is that smile about?" Yasmine probed. Were Zoe's thoughts visible on her face?

She stuffed another strawberry into her mouth.

"It doesn't have to be modern, but it should be sleek!" Zoe's voice was becoming a bit sharp as she and Jules disagreed in front of the cabinet door options at the kitchen furnishings shop. "I still say that looks too village cozy. From what it sounds like with your parents' constant travel, I'm sure your mother likes things simple."

"You've never even met my mother."

Jules remembered the kitchen in the dark apartment he grew up in as being plain, with no particular decorative choices. Just as Agathe had no specialties as a cook. Much of what Jules grew up eating was premade food or picnic items.

Nonetheless, he liked what he liked and thought

the more traditional French country style might add a homey feel. Even if his mother didn't care, at least it could look inviting.

Whereas Zoe favored lacquered lightwood doors without any beveling and brushed nickel hardware. "The tone of the wood is warm," she pressed. "I think that will give you what you're after."

"The client is always right," he quipped with what he knew was a cheeky grin. Zoe rolled her eyes in exasperation. That made Jules chuckle. He nudged it further, "Am I correct?"

Zoe narrowed her eyes like she was regarding him with suspicion.

Which goaded him on. He repeated, "Yes?"

She pointed to a space-age turquoise cabinet door made of plastic. "How about these?" She held her smile for a second to pretend she was serious.

Her determination was admirable, if somewhat exhausting. In spite of himself, he'd become tolerant of their friendly dissimilarities about design. They were on their third disagreement of the day, Jules noted as he looked at his watch. At this rate, the apartment should be completed in five years.

"I'm getting hungry. You don't want me to cross over into *hangry*, do you?" He used the made-up word that signified the shift to anger that lack of nourishment could bring.

"That's because all you drink in the morning is that green goopy concoction. You need something that will stick to your ribs."

"What do you suggest, a pastry?"

"Yes, covered in chocolate," she said with an emphatic nod of her head that made a couple of her curls bounce in the process. Jules still marveled that Zoe's hair had a life of its own, falling this way or that as she moved. "I'm kidding but, you know, an egg, a bowl of warm grains, a yogurt. In short, breakfast."

Words were coming forth from her but he couldn't get his attention off Zoe's mouth as it moved. As a matter of fact, studying her lips was a far more intriguing notion than thinking about the dinner party he had to attend tonight. A large development group from Kenya was visiting the Durand Properties headquarters and meeting with a number of Jules's key people in preparation for a large project in Nairobi.

All the negotiations had been already hammered out, and the evening was just to fete the developers by inviting some of Paris's high society for a dinner cruise on the Seine. Jules loathed that part of his job, the socializing and small talk. He should have invited a date to help chitchat and swat away the gold diggers in glittery dresses who always found their way to him at these things.

Jules had a few female acquaintances in Paris, professionals in the industry who were married to their careers. They knew that Jules wasn't open to anything but occasional companionship. In truth, though, while they were polished and accomplished women, nothing about any of them had sparked his fancy. It felt like too much of a chore to reach out.

After Zoe had checked out the shelving in the back of the store, she walked toward him, biting her bottom lip. Out of nowhere, the desire came over him to nibble on that supple lip himself rather than let her continue do it. How might that plumpness feel between his teeth?

As she moved toward him in what he experienced as

slow motion, he imagined himself sitting at his work desk. And Zoe entering his office, this time not flat on her face from the oopsie she'd taken at their first interview.

Instead, she'd be wearing the close-fitting stretchy black dress she had on today that showcased her compact curves and played nicely against the pale skin of her legs. A devil's deliciousness overtook him when he thought of her striding toward his desk. Toward him. To him. For him. He envisioned himself with a press of a button activating the mechanism that would close all the blinds in his office, giving him total privacy.

The hairs on his arms stood up at the possibility. While Zoe sauntered her way across the office, he'd push his chair back from the desk and beckon her close. His hands would take hold of her hips and pull her to him. With a firm grasp, he'd lift one of her legs around him and then the other, raising her until she sat facing him on his lap, straddling him in his office chair. He'd enjoy exploring the soft flesh in his hands, his pelvis thrusting up to meet her.

As a matter of fact, he fought to prevent his hips from making any motion now, in the middle of the kitchen furnishings shop. Covering his mouth with one hand, he continued to watch Zoe browse in the store, his eyelids at half-mast in his arousal.

In his fantasy, once he'd spent a long leisurely time with the parts of her that were, literally, in reach, his palms would move up her spine. One vertebrae at a time up to the back of her neck where his fingers could finally tangle into that glorious head of hair that he was sure would be as silky and springy as it looked.

Grabbing a fistful of those locks, he'd tilt her head so

that her face was close to his and he'd start feathering light kisses down onto that pretty mouth. That wouldn't hold him for long before he'd begin nibbling little pieces of those lips between his teeth, until he heard a moan of pleasure escape from her throat. At which point he'd kiss her with his full mouth.

Over and over. And over.

Until her lips were red and swollen.

Until…

"Are we getting lunch, or what?" Zoe bounced over, startling Jules with her zest. He felt a strain against the zipper of his pants and casually buttoned his suit jacket to conceal any evidence. She said, "You look hungry."

"I am." She didn't know how right she was.

He instantly refocused, shocked at where his mind had been. He couldn't remember the last time craving had come over him like that. Musing about women wasn't on his agenda. Or never had been, anyway.

It wasn't that Zoe affected him in a way that no other woman had, he told himself. He simply wasn't used to spending so much time with anyone. This was temporary. The apartment would be finished soon enough, his parents would move in and bewitching Zoe would be out of his life. That would be in everyone's best interest.

"I've got a business function to go to tonight," Jules said after he guided them out of the shop and to a market café where they could grab a light bite to hold him until evening. Again, he began to dread being *on* for a boat full of people he barely knew. With no stop for reconsideration, the words fell out. "It's a dinner cruise on the Seine. Are you busy this evening? Would you come with me?"

CHAPTER FOUR

"YOU'RE ASKING ME to come with you for a cruise on the Seine?"

Zoe seemed surprised after Jules invited her to the evening with the Kenyan developers so that he wouldn't have to go alone.

"If you'd like. Some notable people in the Parisian property world will be there, too. You might even make some contacts that could be useful."

There. Jules reframed the invitation in his mind so that it made sense to him. Zoe might benefit from the networking. And he'd be more at ease socializing if he had an ally on his arm. He most definitely did not invite Zoe because he'd just spent a solid fifteen minutes at the kitchen furnishings shop fantasizing about kissing her.

"Oh, well, thank you."

"Are you free?"

"Yep. Nothing on my calendar."

Then why was she hesitating?

"So…is that a yes?"

"I'd be happy to. Only, um…"

"What is it?"

"It's only that…what's the dress code for something like that?"

Ah, so that's what was bothering her.

"I suppose the women will be in cocktail dresses. Do you have something suitable?" Jules could tell that while Zoe had a stylish sort of look, her clothes were clearly inexpensive.

"Maybe you'd rather ask someone else," Zoe said as she busied herself collecting the empty containers on the table from their quick lunch. Gathering everything into her hands, she deposited them in a nearby bin. "You know, more from *your* world."

"*My* world?" Jules knew what she meant but couldn't help mulling it over. Yes, he was acquainted with some of the wealthiest and most prominent residents in Paris. But he enjoyed their company no more or less than he did a construction worker he might talk with in Finland or a waiter in Bangkok.

Jules didn't get close to people. Any people. It didn't matter whether they were rich or poor, buyer or seller, old or young, male or female. Although he knew what Zoe meant about his world, it wasn't one he felt any particular place in. After a boy spends his childhood watching his mother pull a suitcase down the street and finds no ally in his father, he learns to go it alone. Jules only trusted Jules.

Strangely, Zoe, tidying up in her budget but body-hugging black dress, was the first woman he'd ever met that caused him to think twice about all the self-protective decisions he'd made. Not that it mattered, though. She was an employee, not a romantic interest. He didn't have those. She was going to accompany him to a business event. That didn't even count in his three-date policy. Plus, there would never be a second or third to make him question his rules.

"Is the issue that you don't have anything to wear?"

"I don't really go to many dressy occasions."

Jules didn't know a thing about Zoe's background. Whether she'd grown up with money, a childhood that was happy or sad. He knew that she was eager to get the apartment job with him. She'd mentioned that she had a roommate, which made him guess that she leased wherever she lived rather than owned.

"If it's all right with you, I'll buy you a dress. We can pop over to a shop on the Champs-élysées right now."

She whipped her head toward his. "*Pop over* to the Champs-élysées?"

"Yes." He texted Karim to find him a recommendation for a boutique.

"Oh, ho-hum, my boss suggested we *pop* over to buy me a cocktail dress."

A belly laugh erupted in him at her intonation. Jules couldn't remember the last time he'd laughed so heartily. He took her hand and said with a tug, "You're quite something, Zoe Gaiman. Come on, I have other things to finish today besides outfitting you for the evening."

On one of the hallowed side streets off the Champs-élysées, in the area where some of the world's most famous fashion designers had their headquarters, Jules's driver pulled to the curb so that he and Zoe could exit the car. People wearing the latest looks walked this way and that, some chic and on trend, others swallowed up by outrageous clothes that seemed fit only for a runway or featured in a glossy magazine. Tourists intermingled with people whose careers were made or broken on these streets. Fashion was in the air.

In the front windows of their destination, a few dresses hung on bald white mannequins. While they were evening gowns, and more formal than was called for the dinner cruise, Jules approved of their under-stated style. He wanted Zoe to join him for the evening as one of his tasteful young designers, not some flashy arm candy who was going to steal the limelight from his visiting developers.

Karim had phoned the shop ahead of their arrival so they were greeted by the owner as soon as they entered. A tall thin woman with white hair, probably in her sixties, and dressed in a flowing beige outfit introduced herself as Fia.

"Monsieur Durand, it's an honor. How may I assist you today?"

"This is my colleague Zoe. We have a corporate af-fair tonight, a dinner cruise on the Seine. Cocktail at-tire. It may get cold so let's include a wrap. Also shoes and accessories."

"Of course." Fia studied Zoe, no doubt estimating her dress size but also her coloring, height and whatever else she could gleam about her. "May I present some options?"

"Please."

Jules noted the airy boutique. Racks of clothes lined the walls with quite a bit of open space in the center save for a couple of tables where small handbags and sunglasses were displayed. It was a well-curated col-lection, which Jules appreciated, as there was no time to sort through dozens of possibilities.

"Can I offer either of you a glass of champagne?"

"Sure," Zoe wasted no time in answering.

"If you have a mineral water, that would be nice," Jules added.

Fia gestured for them to sit on the sloping black

leather and chrome armchairs that were clustered around a white round coffee table. A previously unseen assistant brought the drinks and then disappeared.

Zoe let out a whistle, then mashed her lips when Fia returned with three dresses. She said, "Let's give these a try. If you'll follow me."

While the ladies departed to, presumably, a fitting room, Jules handled the messages that had come in. There was a voice mail from his father's doctor confirming upcoming appointments. Jules hoped his parents would return to Paris in time to keep them. After a fall down a flight of stairs three years ago broke his back and claimed his mobility, Jules insisted that Hugo be proactive about other facets of his health.

He tagged the message for the file he'd already created called Parents Medical. Others were designated for Residential, Financial and Governmental. If he ran his parents' lives like he ran his business, perhaps he could circumvent the unruly atmosphere he'd grown up in. It was a tall order, but organization was the only thing that kept Jules secure.

Which is why sitting in this dress shop in the middle of the workday suddenly seemed crazy. But not nearly as crazy as that prolonged fantasy he'd had about kissing Zoe and, worse still, the fact that it kept replaying it in his mind. He needed to divert his brain to more productive matters should any future thoughts of that nature arrive.

That affirmation was ticking across his frontal lobe when Fia and Zoe returned to the showroom. Fia had put her in a sleeveless dark orange structural-type dress that had cutouts in the fabric where some sort of mesh was sewn in to cover the flesh that was bared. One slash was across the shoulder while another revealed part of her rib cage, and another still opened across the thighs. It was a creative, fashionable design.

The dark orange color mimicked Zoe's magical hair in a complementary way. But those mesh patches were too sexy. Jules didn't need the extra battle he'd have all evening, trying to avert his eyes from the glimpses of her body under the open weave. Couldn't they just choose something simple and basic?

Fia kept a respectable distance so they could discuss the dress privately.

"I love it," Zoe exclaimed as she approached him, holding her arms outstretched to show off for him.

Her enthusiasm made him want to laugh, like she was the proverbial kid in a candy store.

"Not right for the evening," he stuttered. Deciding not to reveal anything else, he tossed out, "Besides, your exposed bits would get cold. Next."

"Oh, so I don't even get a say," she exclaimed with a cute mock indignation.

"That's right," Jules replied with a wink. A wink! When was the last time he had winked at someone? Never? What was Zoe doing to him?

She returned to the dressing area and then reappeared in the simplest of black dresses with long sleeves and an embroidered band around the high neckline. Boring. Perfect.

"Distinguished," Jules ventured.

"For someone's grandmother." Zoe wrinkled her nose, pivoted and marched back to the fitting room.

While he waited, Jules approved the project schedule for the Miami development. He had several appointments before the cruise and needed to prepare. Hoping the third dress would be the charm, he watched Zoe saunter toward him.

This one was a draped number in a silver metallic fabric. She looked like she was wearing a superhero cape.

"Hate," they both said in unison.

"So, where does that leave us?" He rubbed his palms together. They could continue this all day, actually not an unpleasant proposition, but it really wasn't that important. "Let's get the black…"

"The orange one," Zoe interrupted.

"Fine." Jules could surely control his response to a dress, couldn't he? He waved Fia over and told her of the decision. "Can we outfit her with a coat, shoes, bag… What else do we need?"

"Might I suggest a hair and makeup stylist? Zoe, perhaps you'd like to wear your hair ironed straight for the evening," Fia proposed.

"No, she wouldn't." Both women snapped their heads to glare at him. He must have sounded like an overbearing brute. But he was so enamored of Zoe's nature-defying curly locks that he couldn't stand the idea of them being tamed. Knowing there was nothing he could say to downplay his overreaction, he went for a simple, "I've got to get going. Are we finished here?"

Afterward, he had his driver drop Zoe off at the home decor showroom she wanted to visit for work on the apartment. Jules watched from the car window as she walked away. Shopping had been far more enjoyable than it should have been. Why was doing the most mundane things with Zoe so charged with enthusiasm and vitality? Arguing over a lamp, admiring a purse, seeing her eat a sandwich. As she strode farther away, he inexplicably wished she would turn around and come right back, reclaiming her place beside him in the car. Only when she was finally completely out of view through the window did Jules instruct his driver to pull away.

After the makeup and hair stylist left her apartment, Zoe slipped into the orange cocktail dress and brown stilettos. As long as she lived, she'd never forget the cracked heel that sent her, literally, falling into Jules Durand's office. Navigating a metro station, with all its stairs, in tonight's shoes, would be a recipe for disaster. Fortunately, Jules had sent a car.

Her roommate, Yasmine, wasn't at home so Zoe texted her a quick selfie for feedback on her ensemble. But it was just Zoe and her bedroom mirror to decide if everything was in place. Jules had said a number of influential VIPs in the Paris real-estate scene were going to be in attendance. Making a good impression could lead to jobs that would allow her to stay in Paris. Plus, Zoe had to admit, she wanted to look good for Jules. After all, he'd financed her look from top to bottom.

She couldn't stop thinking about how brusque he'd been when the shop owner, Fia, suggested Zoe straighten her hair for the evening. She had no idea why that had mattered to him but his response had been vehement. And territorial in a way that was shocking at first but very, very, very sexy upon reflection. That take-charge dominance. She'd never met anyone who had such authority over every situation he encountered. Jules's way of doing things was what had brought him success and fortune. He was right to have utter confidence in it.

As to her hair, the stylist had applied several products that accentuated her curls and groomed them into a more tidy pile. A long narrow clip that echoed the slash designs in her dress brought everything together. Reaching for the off-white swing coat that went with the outfit, she reflected on how Jules had made a point to tell Fia that Zoe needed a wrap for the cruise. Yes, it was more evidence of Jules Durand being on top of every little detail, but there was also something so caring about the thought. He didn't want her to get cold. He'd make a fine caregiver to his parents when they returned to Paris.

She had a moment's wonder about his personal life. How many women had Jules made sure didn't suffer an evening chill? She knew from the eligible bachelor lists that he wasn't married and assumed that if there was a woman currently in his life she'd be the one teetering on stilettos to accompany him.

After the driver helped Zoe into the car, she watched out the window as she was whisked through the Paris dusk. It was impossible to say at what hour the city was more beautiful. To her eyes, it was stunning every minute of the day or night. The early evening skies cast a ruddiness on the boulevards as the sun receded. The car crossed over a bridge and Zoe could see the boats of various size and type that were already on the river, most of them with open-air decks and glass-enclosed cabins. Jules's cruise would be joining them shortly.

"You look marvelous," Jules said, as he appeared curbside to usher Zoe out of the car, he and his driver having obviously communicated about her arrival.

"You do, too," she blurted, and then regretted it. But looking good he was, in another exceptional suit. This one was slim-cut and navy, with a navy shirt and a brown tie to match the brown oxford shoes. Everything cut from the finest cloth, constructed with impeccable workmanship and fit to perfection, of course. Zoe couldn't help but take in his personal panache. As she'd thought during every encounter with him, Jules was the most striking man she'd ever seen. It took effort not to swoon.

"Shall we?" They walked a short distance to the dock. He crooked his arm for her to take as he helped her onto the boat's gangway at the riverbank, with the Eiffel Tower as their background. Zoe could hardly believe she was participating in a moment this glamorous. It was like something out of a magazine, dressed-up people on the Seine for an evening ride.

"A pleasure to meet you," Zoe found herself saying over and over again as Jules introduced her to his developers and their significant others who mulled around on the top deck of the luxury boat. The men wore suits and tuxedos while women, both old and young, were dazzling in their fashions and jewels. Bartenders serviced two stations, pouring drinks on order, while waiters passed pretty Kir Royales, champagne tinged with blackcurrant crème de cassis that gave it a red tint. Jules reached for two of the flutes from the silver tray and handed one to Zoe. Hors d'oeuvres were passed on trays lined with flowers and votive candles.

Seating clusters of wooden chairs covered in white sailcloth invited relaxation, but most of the guests stood congregating to keep watch on the Eiffel Tower as the boat pulled away. The captain spoke through a loudspeaker system, pointing out landmarks without sounding too touristy. Audio devices were handed to those who requested translation into other languages.

A thrill overtook Zoe as they passed by the sights, from Les Invalides to the Musée d'Orsay and the Louvre. It was as if she were seeing the Paris attractions for the first time, which she was from the river's view.

She'd be lying if she didn't admit that the moment was profoundly romantic. Paris really was the city for lovers. It wasn't hard to imagine that Jules was her real-life man. That between boat cruises and Michelin-star restaurants and fabulous parties, there was something real and genuine between them. That at the end of every evening out, one more glitzy and exciting than the next, they'd return home to the plush bed they shared where they'd lie down on fine linens to make love and sleep in each other's arms.

Carried away with her musing about Jules really being hers, she barely noticed that she had moved closer to him as he chatted with a guest. Until she distinctly felt her shoulder against his solid arm. She quickly snapped out of it, collected her wits and checked herself and everything around her.

"Do I look like I don't fit in?" Zoe asked Jules once the gentleman he was speaking with stepped away.

"Why do you ask?"

She gestured discreetly with her head at three women across the deck, two blondes and one a brunette, dressed flawlessly from head to toe, all three of their heads craned toward Zoe and Jules. "They keep staring at me."

Jules tipped his flute of Kir Royale in their direction as recognition. "It's not you they're staring at. It's me."

"Why?"

"Haven't you heard? I'm one of Paris's most eligible bachelors," he snickered.

"Oh, my gosh," Zoe quipped. "They're looking at you like you're prey."

"And it feels that way. Nothing but power plays and drama with the likes of them. They're real-estate agents who make plenty of money. But nothing is ever enough. Vultures, indeed."

Zoe decided to inquire on what she'd been curious about. "I take it you're not in a relationship, or else why would you have asked me to accompany you tonight?"

"Most definitely not. Not now and not ever. Three dates is my limit."

He went on to explain about his three-date policy, which was quite sensible, yet the words stung Zoe's face. It wasn't as if she had thought Jules invited her tonight because he was interested in her personally. She knew better than that. He was Jules bloody Durand! He would never date the spunky little designer from Nowhereville.

Not to mention the fact that she was not open to dating, either. There was no way she was ever going to take a chance on adding to the pain that she toted like a piece of luggage. No, thank you. She'd go it alone.

So, she fully understood Jules's three-date rule because it was similar to her body's ping alert system. The little siren that reliably told her she needed to pull back from something that was making her feel.

Yet, somehow, the finality of Jules's declaration about dating was harsh.

The cruise passed by people who sat along the riverbanks eating from picnic baskets, and the sweethearts kissing and waving to the passengers in the boats. Jules shook his head as if in disbelief. "I forget how extraordinary Paris can be."

"I've wanted to live here for as long as I can remember."

"Where were you born?"

Zoe described her hometown of Maupont. "The air
is clean. People look out for each other. But it's a relic.
A couple of historic churches that draw some tourists.
Otherwise, nothing ever happens there."

"Did you visit Paris when you were growing up?"

"Just once as a child. And then I came with friends
as a teenager. My parents had the furniture shop to run
and weren't much for the city. Until they planned their
dream trip to Milan when my brothers and I were older
and could manage the store for them."

"Did they enjoy Milan?"

"They never got there."

"Why?"

"Look at that." Zoe pointed to a building with an
especially elaborate facade. Now was not the time to
have brought up her parents. She'd tell Jules about them
sometime. But she couldn't take a chance of getting
emotional tonight in front of his guests.

"So you decided you wanted to move here…" Jules
sensed that she was withholding something and was
savvy enough to allow her a segue.

"This probably sounds crazy but it all started with a
sofa." Zoe was grateful to move on to another conversation. "A metal-framed sofa covered in a bluish-gray
textural tweed modeled after a style from the 1950s."

"You came to Paris on a sofa?" Had he picked up that
she was on the verge of tears and was trying to lighten
the mood? "Most people use a car. An airplane. Or a
magic carpet."

Zoe smiled and peered up to meet his dark eyes that

glistened in the night sky, as reflective as the moon's illumination on the river. What stunning eyes they were. Observant and thoughtful, yet that spark of playfulness that was dying to pry free was evident in their center. His eyes might be one of her favorite sights in Paris, although she'd keep that vote to herself.

"I loved that one sofa we had at the shop so much. My dad put it in the window display with a complementary side table and lamp. It was what got me interested in interior design. I used to imagine creating a whole room, a whole mood around that one piece. To me, it was elegance and flair. I conjured up a lifestyle that went with that sofa. I was devastated when someone bought it."

"And that led you to Paris?"

"In a way, yes. Once I knew I was going to be a designer, I wanted to be in the capital of style. Where else?"

"So wishes do come true."

Zoe let that dangle. She didn't want to tell Jules that it was only because he'd given her the apartment job that she had any hope of staying at all. That she hadn't been able to break in to the industry in a sustainable way. And that she was one paycheck away from having to go back to the furniture shop where, when last she visited, her brothers had put an ugly dining table and chairs in the shop window instead of another beautiful sofa like the one that had inspired her so.

"Now, of course, I want to visit all of the great sights in the world. Where's your favorite place?"

He contemplated the question for a long time. Zoe wondered why his answer was delayed. "Here," he finally stated. "I've been away for so long I'd forgotten how there's something breathtaking around every corner."

The captain announced that dinner was being served. As the guests chose one of the four staircases leading down to the glass-enclosed dining cabin, Zoe was stunned at the lavish appointments. Gleaming polished wood and shiny brass met her at every turn. The dining tables were dressed in iridescent tan-colored tablecloths and white flower centerpieces twinkled with taper candles arranged at different heights. Charger plates at each diner's place were made of copper and the several forks and spoons at every setting promised a multi-course meal. Likewise, four different-shaped stem glasses per guest meant that the wine had been carefully chosen.

Jules sat Zoe beside him and, after the waiters poured the first wine, stood to offer a welcoming toast that earned him polite applause. The starter course was served, smoked salmon atop a cucumber and artichoke confit, drizzled with herbed cream. It was delicious. Over the dulcet improvisations of the jazz trio that entertained from a small stage, Zoe did a respectable job of hobnobbing with the spouse of one of the developers seated on her other side. She wanted advice on where to shop for purses in Paris. Certain that the stately older woman was not interested in the bargain stores she and Yasmine combed through, Zoe mentioned some high-end shops she'd heard of.

The captain told guests that they were passing under the Pont Neuf—the new bridge. Which was a misnomer, he explained, as it was actually the oldest standing bridge in Paris. He pointed out that the structure had twelve arches and, in addition to the equestrian sculpture of Henry IV, almost four hundred stone mascarons adorning the cornices, their grotesque faces originally thought to keep away evil spirits.

During the entrée, which was a choice of spice-rubbed lamb and Greek quinoa or tart Provençal with wild mushrooms, the captain gave a history of Notre Dame. The cheese course followed, a lovely composition on the plate of three varieties and thick triangles of dense grainy bread dotted with dried fruits. After the boat reached its designated turnaround, the captain continued, relaying information about the Place de la Concorde, the Grand Palais and other sights along the route. As stunning as all those locations had been to Zoe when she'd stood in front of them on the street, under the night sky in the boat's glass cabin she felt like she was in a magical place that only existed in dreams. Not to mention the handsome vision sitting beside her.

Dessert and liqueurs were served buffet-style on the upper deck to better enjoy the final landmarks of their cruise. When Jules left Zoe's side to pay special attention to important clients, she had a pleasant conversation with a couple of Paris developers about utilizing small urban spaces. She hoped she'd made some sort of positive impression so that if she were ever to contact them via a reference from Jules, they would remember her.

After the individual almond cakes with apricot buttercream filling topped with warm dark chocolate sauce, the captain began his return to the riverbank. Just as the clock struck eleven o'clock, the boat faced the Eiffel Tower, obviously perfectly timed for the passengers to best see the hourly light display. With the drama that only Paris could incite, the entire tower began to flicker with golden sparkles, shimmering, glittering and as brilliant as a multi-faceted diamond. It was a spectacle to astonish even the most cynical. Like a woman who throws her shoulders back and owns her beauty, the proud monument twinkled. Everyone on the boat, on the banks and, indeed, from views all over the city halted in time to gape.

Jules stood beside her. Zoe almost thought she could see the reflection of the tower in his eyes. With some sort of knowing smile, they acknowledged that they were sharing a moment. Together.

"So we've found something we agree on," Jules said as he led Zoe off the cruise boat toward his waiting car.

"Paris," she answered with a sweeping arm gesture.

His driver opened the passenger door and they both slid into the back seat.

"Are you tired?" Jules asked her.

"Not too tired. Why?"

"Shall I show you some buildings I love?"

"Do you own them?"

"You may be surprised to know that I don't actually own all of Paris."

"Well, there are always career goals."

Jules shook his head at his cheeky companion.

He rattled off a few landmarks to his driver who dutifully nodded.

First was the Musée d'Orsay, which they'd caught a look at from the boat. Jules lowered the car window and pointed to it. "This is my absolute favorite building in Paris."

"Yes, it's amazing."

"It was originally a railway station done in the beaux arts style."

"Talk about renovating and repurposing."

"Apparently, in the 1970s it was scheduled to be torn down before someone came up with the plan to turn it into a museum."

"Thank goodness." Zoe pointed at the building. "How the structural metalwork integrates with all of the ornate details. Incredible."

"When the barrel-vaulted main space and the train platforms were sectioned off with walls inside to hang the art, museum critics hated it at first. They said the building competed with the art."

Jules was enjoying this, chatting with Zoe. Even though he moved fast and accomplished more in a day than others did in a week, a part of him was numb. There was a switch that had never been flipped to the On position. Zoe was in sharp contrast. Her enthusiasm for everything in front of her was such a breath of fresh air, so alive and unfamiliar.

He wondered why Zoe's parents never boarded that train to Milan. She'd changed the subject when he'd asked about it on the cruise. Did they split up? As a child, he often wished his own parents would, although he was never sure which one of them would be worse to live with. Navigating around both of them had taken up so much of his focus from as far back as he could remember.

When his mother was away on her pointless desertions, young Jules would look out the sooty window of their dank apartment on its ugly and nondescript block as if he were searching for her. Or stare, mystified, at the dirty laundry and unmade beds. He worried it was his fault that she'd left, clearly she wasn't a nurturer like most mothers were. He resented his father's inability to put a halt to the situation, or to comfort his son, and considered him weak. Jules never felt loved and never learned to love in return.

He became an angry young man and channeled his rage into becoming hyper-structured, planning out everything from what he was going to wear the next day to how he was going to acquire his next property. He found an ironic comfort in controlling what he could in his life.

After amassing extreme wealth, he started to send money to his parents. He knew it was wrong, that the child should not have to support the mother and father, but he did it anyway as his fortunes grew to the point that the expense had no impact. Blood was blood and he considered it his duty.

When he thought of it all right now, sitting next to vivacious Zoe while they drove through the storied boulevards of the city center, Jules felt a hole in his gut. He was becoming painfully aware that with his chosen lifestyle, he was missing out. That he wasn't leading a full existence, one that deserved some happiness and heart song.

There had to be more than being a parent to parents who were never even good to him, with whom he shared no pleasant memories to coast along on. And more than making billions of euros, most of which sat compounding into more money in never-used investment accounts. The word *enjoyment* had never been on Jules's radar. He was starting to see that if he didn't lighten up inside, darkness was going to cloud over him.

"Now, this works. But how?" Zoe marveled as they approached Centre Pompidou in the Fourth Arrondissement, which snatched his attention back to the present. The high-tech architecture, with its inside-out style where the mechanical systems such as plumbing and electrical were exposed and color-coded on the outside of the building, was one of a kind.

"Some people think it's a monstrosity," he said of the structure that was part art museum, part library and part event space.

"It's a fine line between what works and what doesn't when you do modern on a big scale like this."

"Good point."

Jules was so glad he'd brought Zoe along on the cruise tonight. It was meeting her that had set his mind to wondering about pleasure and about dark shadows. About sharing sunsets. He'd never met a woman he could imagine having a longstanding companionship with, and would never take the chance of ending up in a rancorous union like his parents. Yet, he had to admit the idea of attachment to someone had been crossing his mind, especially in the past few days.

With his face still close to Zoe's as she peered out the window at the Pompidou, he chose instead to study those orange ringlets of her hair up close. They really were a miracle from another realm. Her brain must be filled with some magical powers.

Entranced by a woman's curl?

Yes, Jules definitely needed to bring some diversion into his life. Maybe he should take up tennis.

And what about that dress? He cut his eyes to steal a glimpse of the slash across the shoulder. The design was clever in how it revealed the shapeliness of her décolleté. The hair, the sexy dress, Zoe's peppy companionship at dinner, it had all worn him down. The hour was late and Zoe's seductiveness overtook him. Craving became need before he could restrain it.

As the driver pulled away from the Centre, Zoe turned her head toward Jules, presumably to say something.

Which he didn't allow because before she could speak he leaned over, brought his lips to hers and delivered a long melting kiss. It was better than anything he could think of that had happened in the recent or distant past.

CHAPTER FIVE

IN AN INSTANT, Zoe was pulled under into a warm and pleasant universe where all she could feel or taste was Jules. While she was able to discern that only their lips were actually touching, it felt like he was all over her, like together they'd merged into one being and she didn't know where she began and he ended. Then, abruptly, he blurted, "My apologies," and jerked backward to his proper place in the car's back seat.

He'd previously instructed his driver to take them to Montmartre, where Jules was intending to show her some notable buildings. With a hand flat against his chest, he emphasized, "How utterly inappropriate. I don't know what I was thinking. I'm so very sorry."

Zoe stilled. Not a cell of her was able to move. She was stuck in an unnatural position, half turned toward the man who had just laid his lips on hers, yet her hips were twisted the opposite direction from looking out the window. Although her brain told her to straighten out, her body wouldn't cooperate.

She'd been hoping to make another clever comment about the architecture Jules was showing her but the words weren't able to make it out because he had covered her mouth with his. His lips had obviously delivered some type of paralyzing potion because all she could do was look into his eyes, perhaps waiting for an explanation. And listening to that constant ping inside her chest confirmed that her emotions were exposed for the plucking. Like plump, ripe fruit from a tree.

"That's okay-ay," she stuttered, adding an extra syllable to her simple words. Zoe most definitely wasn't *okay-ay* but she felt she should say something. Jules looked so pained, the furrows between his eyebrows digging in.

Jules Durand, *the* Jules Durand, had just kissed her, and making billion-euro real-estate transactions was not all he was good at. His kiss was masterful. He slid effortlessly from paper soft to insistent to erotic. From sweet to spicy, nice to naughty. It went on for hours. Okay, it was minutes but it felt like a week. As he finally, abruptly, stopped, Zoe wanted more, internally screaming with a tormenting deficit when he yanked himself away. It was a kiss she would remember forever. And despite his apologies, the kiss hadn't been forced upon her, if that was something he was worried about. No, as soon as the sensation of his firm lips against hers registered, she'd sunk into it, and gave as much as she'd received.

"I promise you that will never happen again," Jules rasped, clearing his throat. "You know I don't generally act in the spur of the moment."

"Of course," she replied in a monotone. "Neither do I." Obviously, it had been a mistake. They were colleagues and nothing more.

So why did his promise that kissing her would never happen again smart like a rejection? Maybe because Zoe hadn't been on a date in a long time and Jules's touch ignited dormant embers of desire that had been smoldering deep within her. She'd had a few dates in Maupont, but no one had ever activated the ping. Not like he just had.

She had to remind herself that even if Jules had any interest in her, which he didn't beyond as an employee, no serious liaisons were in her future. Funny that around him she kept forgetting that decision.

Uneasiness permeated the car like a strange scent as the driver continued whisking them down one street and then another, traffic eased in the late hour. Jules sat up very straight and kept his eyes forward. Zoe finally summoned the ability to adjust her body to face the front, as well.

After a few minutes of traveling in silence, Jules used his matter-of-fact voice. "Zoe, I've noticed that you are a very…what's the word…enthusiastic person."

"Is that a polite criticism of some sort?" She resisted the urge to swivel her head toward him so they spoke with all four eyes focused out the car's front window, privacy glass still separating them from the driver.

"Not at all. I admire it. I've been calculating that the amount I work coupled with what will be my new responsibilities with my parents won't leave a lot of time for…recreation?"

"You mean work and life balance?"

"Work and life balance, yes. Work has been my life. There is no balance."

"So, what do you do for fun?"

"Fun?" He scratched his chin as he contemplated the question.

"To relax, to decompress."

"That was fun."

"What was fun?"

"Kissing you just now. That was fun."

Yeah, she'd have to agree. It was birthday-party-with-triple-layer-cake-and-candles fun locking her lips with his.

"Maybe you should try it more often," she suggested tentatively, not sure if she was being flirted with.

"No. Most definitely not. Kissing, romance, all of that is not an option. What do you think of golf?"

After Jules had his driver take Zoe home, she slipped the key through the lock to her apartment door.

"Yowza!" Yasmine exclaimed as she came in. Zoe's roommate wore red pajamas covered with a graphic design of puppies and she ate ice cream with a spoon straight from a large container. "You look ah-may-zing."

Zoe kicked off the stilettoes that had been killing her but were worth it for the stature they'd given her. After falling into Jules's office, she'd vowed never to wear heels again but the dress Jules had bought her for the cruise seemed to beg for the extra zhoosh. She'd sent a selfie earlier but apparently the ensemble was even better in person. Yasmine leered at her from top to bottom.

"The dress worked, that's for sure," Zoe reported. "I felt good in it and you should have seen me hobnobbing with Parisian VIPs! I can really talk the talk. Maybe something will come of it."

"What about you and the billionaire?"

She wasn't sure that she should tell anyone, even her roommate, about Jules's accidental kiss that would have no meaning tomorrow. Zoe did not want to be quizzed on every move made by Jules Durand.

"There's nothing going on there. He's my boss. I didn't embarrass him so I'd call the evening a success."

"Were there other attractive men there?" Yasmine snooped before spooning a big bite of ice cream into her mouth.

There might have been handsome men in attendance, after all this was Paris and there was the Kenyan contingent as well, but Zoe had failed to notice. She'd barely taken her eyes off Jules other than to exchange pleasantries with the guests he'd introduced her to. They'd been side by side most of the evening. In fact, when he stepped away to greet someone or get a drink, she'd felt the empty space beside her whoosh like a chill.

Zoe took a spoon from the drawer and dug into Yasmine's ice cream for a scoop. She asked wistfully before tasting it, "Have you noticed that this city is a really romantic place?"

"Are you kidding me?" Yasmine scrunched up her face.

"Sometimes I wish I was in love with more than just sofas and paint colors."

"Aha, so maybe a certain someone is making you rethink your no-serious-relationship rule."

"Hardly," Zoe answered too quickly. "In fact, he himself has a *three-date* rule, which I think is very sensible." She explained Jules's rubric.

"Uh-huh," Yasmine replied unconvincingly and licked her spoon.

Zoe had a full day's work on the apartment ahead of her in the morning, so she changed out of the dinner outfit, washed up and went straight to bed. Except that sleep didn't come. Lying on her back and staring up at a shadow across the ceiling, both her body and her brain still vibrated.

Darn Jules for planting that delicious kiss on her! Because even though he retracted it with his words, Zoe's lips were still reacting. How, in a blink, his kiss had sent sensations up and down her like hot blood that coursed through veins parched from drought.

His kiss kindled mental portraits of lovers in Paris. Walking arm in arm, appreciating every bridge over the shimmering river. Strolling down a boulevard, gesturing and animated in their conversations, so much to tell each other. Those same lovers admiring a painting, sharing a pastry, kissing in a dusty bookshop, unable to contain their need for one another. And once they got home, exploring the depths of their desire until the raw sunlight of dawn opened the skies.

Why did Jules have to kiss her? Now Zoe couldn't stop whirling about possibilities she'd forbidden herself to dwell on. She knew herself enough to be sure that she was a person who loved wholly and fully, so casual encounters were never going to do for her. It was all or nothing, and she'd chosen the latter. It wasn't helpful to have her resolve put to the test.

In that way, she was a little like Jules. Having a plan. To protect her heart. And in a strange fashion, tonight he had behaved like her. His kiss was on impulse. Had he thought about it, he certainly wouldn't have done it. Instinct propelled him to her. Instinct was what Zoe usually relied on. What was happening?

That. That was fun.

Jules's earlier statement resonated between her ears.

She scolded his words inside her head to be quiet and to let her fall asleep. Instead, the voice got louder.

Kissing you was fun.

Fun. What a stupid word Jules had used, he reflected during his morning run. He was a thirty-four-year-old billionaire. Obviously, he didn't get this far this quickly in life by having fun. Children in a playground had fun. Frivolous party girls in tiny dresses at nightclubs had fun. Carefree heirs to fortunes lolled about on yachts having fun. Jules worked. Thought. Worked some more.

As was his usual routine for his run, he briskly walked for two blocks in order to loosen up and get his circulation flowing. For the next two, he brought himself to a light jog. Then he stopped for his sequence of muscle stretches to prevent injury. Once he was fully warmed up, he increased his speed to a run and, before long, his breathing rose to meet the exertion.

Images flickered through his mind. Morning runs in the sweltering humidity of Manila. Through the bite of a Chicago winter's dawn. Along beaches in Maui. Yes, he had business in every corner of the earth. He'd toured historic sights. Tasted unique foods. Participated in extreme sports. Been awed by natural wonders. Had interludes with beautiful women. But had he found any *fun*?

This was where he'd take his morning run now. Under the unmistakably Paris skies. These streets were to be his permanent neighborhood, his home turf. Was there *fun* around any of these city corners? What exactly was *fun*, anyway?

Kissing Zoe was *fun*. There was no way he could deny that, even though his brain struggled for a more academic understanding of the word. It was an unfortunate accident that he'd now have to correct by never letting it happen again. He'd told her as much when he apologized for acting on a whim. What was it about her that had propelled him to make that move without self-intervention?

Jules rounded another corner. His breath had reached heaving and he welcomed the perspiration. He checked the fitness settings on his watch to make sure his speed and heart rate were in target range.

Zoe was an underling who'd escorted him to a business function. There wasn't anything personal between them. They hadn't even known each other long enough to be called friends. Absolutely nothing could have predicted that he would claim her mouth like that, fixing his lips to hers until they both had to come up for air.

In all honesty, it wasn't entirely unprecedented. There was that steaming hot fantasy about Zoe striding across his office in her black dress and straddling him in his office chair. When he envisioned his hands grabbing onto everything they could reach as their lips collided in a forbidden middle-of-the-work-day merge that would have shocked his employees on the other side of the glass if they knew what was happening behind closed blinds. Were that little daydream to have come to life, he and Zoe would have spent time on his expensive carpeting, and it wouldn't have been because of a broken shoe.

He hadn't given those images a second consideration. Well, maybe, he hadn't given them a fifth. Or was it a fifteenth? In any case, when she asked him in the back seat of the car what he did for pleasure, apparently he'd shown her. A smile crossed his lips at the recollection, and he lifted the bottom of his T-shirt to wipe the sweat from his face as he finished his run.

After showering, he sipped the green drink the housekeeper had left. Reading over some reports for the condo development in Krakow that was frustrating him with budget overages, his mind kept drifting back to Zoe's sweet lips.

Fun.

Kissing her in the car, he'd acted without premeditation. There was another word he'd been contemplating. *Spontaneity.* Something unplanned. Occurrences that had no place in his world and could, by their very nature, only lead to mistakes. Like kissing Zoe, in case he needed any proof. Worse still, he feared that what he was feeling was more than a sexual charge from his encounter with her lovely mouth and his musings on what her body might feel like in his hands. There was a knocking inside of his gut, like some sort of wake-up call.

He was fighting to ignore it.

Jules didn't need anything more to deal with. For so long without a place he had called home, he'd been able to board intercontinental flights and jet away from any longing that might have made its way under his skin. From uncertainties that had started popping up more and more frequently, about connection and priorities. Contemplations he couldn't shut down.

It was harder here. Jules had never been a lover in this city that celebrated them. He'd spent the occasional carnal night or weekend with one of the exotic women he'd met in faraway locales. Superficial encounters that happened between people who would never meet each other again. After which it was easy to say goodbye.

As he knotted his tie and collected his things for work, that increasingly persistent nagging came at him again, telling him that it was no longer enough.

Grabbing his attaché case and other belongings, he stepped out his door, vowing to stop thinking about saying good morning to Zoe—every morning—for the rest of his life.

"I've been invited to Prague with a lovely family I met who are in need of childcare," Agathe's shrill voice pierced through Jules's phone when he and Zoe were at the apartment a few days later. He stepped into the kitchen out of earshot and left Zoe in the living room.

"Oh, good heavens, Mother." He could only imagine what lies she'd told this family to get them to believe she was capable of looking after children.

"It's not as if your father would care if I…" The strength in Agathe's voice faded, as if she herself were tired of her own script. Jules certainly was.

His loud exhale contained particles of disgust. It was as if a recording that they'd both heard a thousand times was playing. "You are not going to Prague."

"I hate him," she squawked feebly.

"Yes, Mother, I know. You always hate him until you don't." Love was ridiculous. The universe was giving him another reminder to steer clear of it. "Stop this nonsense and get on the plane to Paris."

Jules ended the call and returned his attention to Zoe. She had brought some paint samples and brushed one swath of each color onto the wall. While he really didn't know her well, he could tell that she wasn't like his mother with inconsistent mood swings and a general bitterness, as if life owed her something that it wasn't delivering.

What kind of mother would a woman like Zoe be? Yes, the type who takes her kids to the park and then buys them an impromptu ice-cream cone, eliciting more delight than a planned snack would. But would she also know how to put boundaries on that impetuosity, to raise children who learned how to focus on school exams and work diligently toward goals?

Jules had long ago decided that he'd help the population by not bringing more children with unfit parents into the world. After the instability he grew up in, he was convinced he'd go too far in the other direction and be a controlling and regimented father.

Letting the paint dry, next Zoe analyzed the lighting that had been installed in the hallway that led to the bedrooms and bathroom.

"I wonder if we could better mimic natural morning light with some additional overheads here. Since we haven't painted yet, it wouldn't be too big a job to add on. Let me think on that." She sat down cross-legged on the bare floor in the middle of the hallway. She slowly looked around her, panning side to side, then up and down, as if there was some new information to be gleamed. *Feeling it.* Like she was summoning the dead to vote in.

"Are you conducting a séance?"

"No. But that's a great suggestion. Let me consult my tarot cards. And what are your parents' zodiac signs?"

Jules knew she was joking but his call with his mom had stripped him of any sense of humor he might have been able to muster.

"I have lighting analysis software and you can try your ideas with that," he declared.

He knew his tone was harsh. Still sitting on the floor, Zoe glared up at him. One of her corkscrew curls bounced forward on its own volition and covered one eye. She swept it away with the back of her hand defiantly.

Something in Jules wanted to sit down on the hardwood floor next to her. Maybe take off his shoes. Maybe hold Zoe close. Maybe be in the moment and see what happened.

But he didn't do that sort of thing.

Instead, he offered an olive branch. "Can I take you to dinner?"

The cruise on the Seine was date number one. Except it hadn't been a date because it was a business function. The kiss afterward was a freak accident and he'd already apologized for his mistake. The quick lunches they'd grabbed definitely didn't get logged. Tonight would be date number two, only it wouldn't count, either, as they would be discussing the apartment. It was all figured out. There would not be any more physical contact. Although, dinner would bring him dangerously close to date number three, should they need to spend another evening together in the future. If one was counting these things.

"What do you think of the medium-blue paint?" She stood and led him back into the living room.

"It's bold but the room can take it."

"Jules, did you just make a decision based on preference?" This time she got him to crack a smile. "You'll find it shocking to know that I consulted a color-scheme program. Warm colors advancing and cool colors receding and all those *rules* you like so much."

"Aha! What did that lead you to?"

"Well, at first I was thinking that everything needed to be soothing. Perhaps it's a day that your parents are out and about in the intensity of the city. That they need a gentle cocoon to come home to."

"And then?"

"Then I thought that maybe a home with verve and energy was better for globe-trotters. One that was stimulating in its own right. So I came to this." She pointed to the paint swatch on the wall. "A much darker blue than I would have expected to try. With the main decor colors being forest green, rust and khaki. Something about that feels like the colors of travel."

"Colors of travel? There you go *feeling* again."

"Since they've done so much of it."

"Hmm."

From what Zoe knew, his parents' endless journey was enviable, not a rootless search for belonging and contentment that the Durand family apparently knew nothing about.

"You can't deny that you still have to respond to the suggestions a software program lays out. There are still subjective..."

Jules grabbed Zoe's hand and pulled her toward the front door. "Let's go eat and we can see how the paint colors *feel* to me in tomorrow's light."

Jules led them around one corner and then another and then another, which put them on pedestrian-only Rue Montorgueil in the First Arrondissement. Known as an international foodie paradise, the cheese shops, fishmongers, patisseries and restaurants serving food from every corner of the world beckoned.

After much discussion, they chose a bustling Thai restaurant and took two seats side by side at the counter facing the open kitchen. Zoe opened her laptop and called up a lighting placement program to show him the changes she wanted to do.

"Comes in handy, doesn't it?" he teased again about her use of the computer-aided design, raising an eyebrow in a mock-gloating manner that was adorable. She begged herself to stop reminiscing about that kiss the other night, the one he'd promised never to repeat. Yet, she found herself wishing he would.

If only he wasn't sitting so close to her. Shoulder to shoulder, they both occasionally looked up to watch the chefs in front of them flipping noodles over scorching high heat, the finished products lush with jewels of diced meats and colorful vegetables.

Jules's long muscular arm pressed against hers as they huddled over the laptop screen. Her whole being buzzed when she was close to him. And as they dug into their delicious pad Thai, the rich peanut flavor somehow added to the sensuality. It was a combination of sensations that made her almost light-headed, and had the power to make the loud and crowded restaurant fade into the distance of her consciousness. Zoe wanted to lick the sweet sauce from Jules's lips. Wanted to drop into his arms and press herself against his solid chest. Wanted them to hold onto each other like there was no tomorrow. No one on earth had ever made her feel that way. She hoped nobody ever would. It was really too much.

"I'm not a fool," Jules said as they took a stroll after

dinner. "I know that there's an artistic element to what you do. If I didn't appreciate that, I wouldn't need a designer. I'd simply let the computer make all of the decisions."

They approached the nearby Musée du Louvre. Closed for the evening, crowds still mulled about photographing the world's most famous museum under the moon's glow. Originally a castle, with construction that began in the twelfth century, it became a museum in the 1700s. The campus, its enormous main courtyard and the glass-and-steel pyramid that stood at its center, was instantly recognizable.

"You told me you fell in love with design via a sofa. Did you take art history in school?" Jules asked.

"Of course."

"What kind of child were you?"

Zoe gulped. It was still hard for her to discuss anything about her past without missing her parents so much that the anguish threatened to knock her to the ground. "I suppose I was a happy enough kid. As much as you can be with three older brothers."

"Was your parents' furniture shop successful?"

"Define *success*."

"Touché."

"They made a living in a small town where there wasn't much opportunity. They were in love, so I'd define that as succ…" Her lower lip quivered uncontrollably, leaving her unable to complete the sentence.

"What is it?"

Zoe dabbed away the tears that clouded her vision as they got closer to the pyramid. "One of the last things my mother ever said to me before my parents died was that she hoped I'd someday meet someone as wonderful as my father."

"Your parents died? At the same time? Was there an accident?"

She'd forgotten that she hadn't told Jules about her parents' fate and did so now. "One day they were unlocking the shop door in the morning, turning the old-fashioned sign from Closed to Open and then back to Closed at the end of the day. You go through the motions, thinking you've eked out an existence, that you can count on, that you're content." The ping in her chest hurt so much it could have been a knife blade. "And in the next moment they were gone."

"Oh, my gosh," he responded. "That's an unimaginable tragedy."

"Maybe it's what turned me into the adult I am. I've become one of those *seize life* kind of people, but really it's that I have to be because I'm terrified it can all be taken away in a flash."

"So that's why you're not a planner."

"Touché back to you." She looked out to the courtyard. "There's one thing I'm very organized about. My mom was wrong about wanting me to meet the right person. I'm never going to be with a partner."

"Because they might die?"

Zoe was surprised at Jules's bluntness. Although that was something she liked about him, his way of cutting through to the quick of something.

"Yeah. What are the odds of dying at the same time as the love of your life? Pretty low. So that means there's a fifty percent chance of them dying before you."

"This from a person who says she doesn't bring mathematic systems into her life."

At the base of the Louvre Pyramid, they cranked their necks back to take it in from bottom to top, in unabashed awe.

"What about you, with your three-date rule? Talk about structured."

"I witnessed something very different growing up. Chaos. I can't have that in my life."

"So women equal disorder?"

"Something like that. In any case, it's much easier not to take chances."

"We're on the same page about that. You don't go on fourth dates and I don't get close to anyone."

"Bravo for us. We've figured out our own safety nets."

They both laughed into the night, pretending to be so pleased with themselves.

CHAPTER SIX

"Agathe and Hugo, this is my associate, Zoe Gaiman," Jules introduced his parents in the lobby of the Juin Hotel, a boutique inn he owned on the Left Bank. The black-painted exterior outside with its silver awning displaying the hotel name led to the smart interior.

The black-and-white-tiled floor complemented the wallpaper with its design of black pineapples, the fruit a historic symbol of hospitality. Jules had been very pleased when this hotel had gone up for sale a couple of years ago and he'd been able to purchase it. It had been in operation for seven decades.

Zoe shook Agathe's limp hand and bent gracefully down to shake Hugo's from his seat in the wheelchair.

"Jules, you didn't tell us you were seeing someone," Agathe exclaimed in her overly dramatic manner. He hadn't seen her theatrics in person for a while and thought she grew sillier and sillier with age.

"I'm not dating anyone, Mother. As I just mentioned, Zoe is my colleague. She's a talented designer who's assisting me in readying the apartment for you."

"Colleague," Agathe repeated with hiked eyebrows. She retrieved a lace handkerchief, as if something from another century, from her small handbag and used it to blow her nose. Hugo's pallor was gray.

Jules was surprisingly relieved to have Zoe come along for the reunion with his parents, especially after he'd told her more about his childhood, more than he'd ever told anyone. He tallied up just how much time he'd been spending with her. Oddly, the realization didn't displease him. He'd felt comfortable asking her to come along for moral support, although he didn't voice that in as many words.

When he refused to send more money to his parents in Tel Aviv and Agathe's scheme to become a Prague nanny had fallen through, he'd finally squeezed them enough financially to the point where they had no choice but to use the plane tickets he'd provided.

It had been six months since he'd last seen them. On a trip west from Dubai, Jules had stopped in Hungary where they were working as models for a painter who was doing a study on older bodies.

Just the sort of thing his mother had spun into a grandiose tale of adventure, the reality was that the artist in question lived in poverty on a barely operational farm and wasn't paying them a salary. They slept on a haystack in a barn and fetched their eggs every morning from underneath a chicken. When Jules arrived, he found them with dirty bare feet and his father exhausted by a persistent dry cough. Not exactly how seniors, one with health issues no less, should be spending their time.

It was then he'd decided that enough was enough, that he'd need to take charge and prevent any more bad decisions. He needed to look out not only for their well-being but also for their safety.

Had he found them happy and taking good care of themselves, he might have been willing to let them continue their endless drifting. After all, they didn't need employment. He could certainly afford to finance their wanderings. But his father was drinking too much and his mother was, as always, belittling and threatening to desert him, even though it had been years since she actually had. She no longer had the adeptness to run away on her own like she had in years past.

"You're coming home where we'll see proper doctors and you'll live as respectable Parisians," Jules had proclaimed at the painter's farmhouse. "I'm not going to receive a phone call from some remote corner of the world to find out you've been eaten by wild animals or have starved to death."

After that endless row in Tel Aviv, the time had finally come. He'd house them at this hotel until the apartment was ready.

"Monsieur Durand, may I show your parents to their suite?" The hotel manager, who wore a suit and tie with a name tag adorning his jacket's lapel, joined the group.

"Thank you, Huy."

Two bellmen appeared to handle the luggage.

"Zoe." Jules placed his hand on the center of her back to escort her toward the elevator. He wasn't expecting his palm to be greeted with the plushness of the baby pink sweater she wore that seemed to promise something even softer underneath. He supposed it was only natural that his mother would have immediately assumed that Zoe was a romantic interest. That the thought wasn't repugnant was a first for him.

"Shall I push the chair for you?" Jules offered to his father.

"Obviously, I can do it myself." A bark of an answer—not unexpected. Resentment that Jules was controlling their fates. Had his father planned for his elder years, perhaps he wouldn't have been reduced to that. Jules noticed how brawny Hugo's biceps had gotten from their labors. His father speedily pushed the wheels of his chair until he had gotten halfway across the lobby ahead of the rest of the party.

Jules had a moment of terror over what he was embarking on. Bringing these people back into his life who were, for all intents and purposes, dreadful parents. Was he trying to stage a do-over? Did he think that if he cared for them now it would somehow right all the wrongs, salve all of the hurts? How much control did he *really* have?

Once they arrived at the suite, Jules asked Huy to send up some sandwiches, fruit and juice. "We'll see the orthopedic doctor next week to have you fully evaluated, Father. When was the last time the two of you had a complete physical examination?"

"While you're at it, get your mother a psychological exam," Hugo snapped.

Agathe pretended not to hear him as she inspected the suite. "So this is what my prison cell will look like," she stated without looking at any of them. Jules had overestimated his mother's interest in not embarrassing him. Obviously, civility in front of Zoe, who she'd never met, was of no matter to her. Had Jules known his parents were going to be *this* badly behaved, he wouldn't have brought her to witness it.

Jules's forehead became very tight. A headache was developing and he considered taking some aspirin. He hissed in Agathe's ear, "It's only temporary, Mother. I suppose my elite hotel that's fully booked year-round doesn't have the charm of a Hungarian haystack, but you might actually enjoy indoor plumbing."

"Agathe, have you seen the view?" Zoe called from the window. Jules's mother joined her. They looked out to a pretty street with apartments across the way, all the windows adorned with flower boxes. "Isn't Paris lovely?"

"I lived here for too long, dear," Agathe exhaled. "I'm underwhelmed by a few peonies in some store-bought dirt."

"Mother, stop being so rude."

"Soon enough, we'll have the apartment ready and then you can truly settle into your new home," Zoe persisted. "I hope you'll like all the choices we made."

She was clearly trying to help, and Jules wanted to kiss her for it.

His headache was turning into a throb.

"My electricians are installing your hallway redesign this morning," Jules informed Zoe during a FaceTime session. He'd been busy with his parents and they hadn't seen each other at the apartment for a few days. But each morning, she'd met with him on a video chat. Zoe had to admit she looked forward to the early call and was always dressed and ready for him at the designated time.

She'd be lying if she said he wasn't on her mind, but the distance was an important reminder that after this job was finished she didn't know how frequently they'd be in contact. "I'd like to show you some sketches I had for the bedroom furniture placement."

"Sketches?"

"Yes, Jules." She took on a jokey tone as, by now, their different working methods were no surprise to each other. "I had some ideas after I met your parents last week."

"What sort of ideas? That we'll need armed guards to keep the troops in line at their residence?"

Zoe watched Jules through the screen. He was sitting tall at his office desk, the view expansive behind him even through the screen on her tablet. Although Zoe couldn't say for sure which was a better vista to gaze upon, Paris's rooftops or Jules Durand in his brown suit, white shirt and red tie.

It was shocking to think that Zoe had become a part of this man's high-flying lifestyle. Seeing him on the screen like she was watching a television show, he sipped his thick green breakfast concoction, sorted through papers on his desk and fired off messages from his computer. He was a master class in multitasking. She couldn't help but admire how much Jules got done in a day.

She'd also come to know another side of him. Although he made a joke about his parents needing military peacekeepers, she could recognize in his face, in his posture, in his voice, that he was under a lot of stress. She even saw vulnerability in those dark brown eyes.

Zoe could hardly blame him after what she'd witnessed when meeting Jules's parents at his hotel. His mother was ungrateful and unpleasant and spoke without any kind of self-filter. Hugo wasn't much better. Jules was short with them, already exhausted by his caretaking mission.

The more she thought about it, the more it bothered

her that neither of them said thank-you to Jules. For their plane fare from Tel Aviv. For the hotel suite and upcoming apartment. For any of it. She didn't know all of what had transpired between them but it was enough to make her want to protect him. It was ironic that she wanted to don a suit of armor to defend the big tall billionaire.

Studying him on the video call, Zoe noticed how the clench in his shoulder blades made him look stiff sitting in his chair. Analyzing his striking face, the divots between his eyebrows were the most sunken she'd ever seen them. She figured he hadn't fully fathomed what he was getting himself into by bringing his parents back until they'd actually arrived.

She went ahead and voiced her concern. "Jules, you look tense. Did you go for your run this morning?"

He'd told her that morning exercise was vital to his routine.

"Yes." He took another sip of his drink.

"And you have a busy day full of conferences and acquisitions?"

For the first time during the conversation, he looked directly into her eyes on the screen in response to her semi-sarcastic comment.

"Yes, Zoe. I run an empire, you know. And tense doesn't even begin to describe it."

He was having a hard morning, and she was starting to get the feeling that he had come to consider her someone he could talk to, someone who had something to offer him. That he could be real around her, which was rare for him. There was definitely something inside of him that he needed to release. More than strain. It was like there was another man inside the accomplished one she watched through the screen, one who fit in Paris.

A man with a big romantic passion he kept under the surface. Maybe the city itself could eventually set that free for him. Or maybe she could.

What was the good in that, though? Helping Jules unlock his inner spirit was no concern of hers one way or another. She was never going to be the person he'd share that emancipation with. No one was. He'd made that clear. Although, if she were being honest, the notion had popped up in her mind more than a few times. Especially after that delicious mistake of a kiss, the one she was still replaying. What would it be like to be his lover, his best friend, his wife?

It was hard to picture the man who swore by his three-date rule and had spent most of his adult life living in the world's sleekest hotels, participating in domestic pleasures. Would he look forward to coming home to her at night? A designated hour that work ended for the evening? When they would prepare a home-cooked meal, eaten cozily at their little round table for two? Would he stop at the store on the way home to buy medicine when she called suffering from a runny nose? Might there be a beloved pup curled up at his feet while they watched a movie on a lazy Sunday?

No, he had people who went to the store for him. His life was too busy for a pet. A cute little table for two? Absurd!

"What do you have over there?" he commented on what he was viewing from his end of the FaceTime chat. "Is that a toolbox on your table?"

She explained that the hammer, nails and whatnot had been left out as she and Yasmine were attempting to repair a bedroom dresser they'd found broken and abandoned on the street. "We always need extra storage," she explained. "We're going to sand it down to the original wood and then stain it."

"That's what you do in your spare time? Restore other people's garbage?"

"We've never tried it before."

Zoe absentmindedly touched his cheek on her tablet's screen, as if she could penetrate through all the way to his skin.

"What happened?" He reacted to her movement. "Why did you just touch your screen?"

Oops! "Oops," she covered quickly, having forgotten how that move would appear at his end of the connection. "I was just wiping a smudge." While she'd been staring at his face as he spoke to her, it was as if his likeness on the screen rather than in person gave her license to let out some of her own bubbling emotions.

She'd become deeply attracted to him. No doubt about it. What she had initially found irritating about him, she'd come to respect. He'd been able to channel his organizational and decision-making skills into a billion-euro corporation, in spite of an upbringing that offered no encouragement. What he was willing to do for his parents, out of duty and not because they deserved it, was noble. He was a force for good in a world that needed it.

And she wanted to peel away more of his outer layers, to set free the fiery man that she kept getting glimmers of. Glimmers that were keeping her awake at night, so compelling were the *what-ifs* her brain was now constantly ticking with. What if she herself was open to romance, to love? One thing she knew for sure was that if she were, she'd want to be with Jules.

Zoe had been convincing herself for so long now that

she would never enter into a serious relationship. In fact, terror gripped her at the mere thought of something happening to Jules, and they weren't even together.

After her parents' instant deaths, Zoe was despondent for months. The pain of having both parents taken at the same time was a hurt so savage it had the strength to tear her apart limb by limb. She thought she'd never rise up from the sorrow, from the grief.

It was like walking in a daze for a couple of years. To lose her parents was bad enough, but in such a shocking way was too much to overcome.

When she finally did emerge, the lack of opportunity in Maupont was unbearable. She needed change. One day, she visited the cemetery where her parents and grandparents were buried. She had a heart-to-heart chat with them at their gravesites and asked them what to do. It was then she realized she had to come to Paris. She had to pursue her ambition. And at the same time, she decided firmly she could never accept the unknown that getting close to someone would bring. Therefore, she'd avoid it completely.

So it made no sense at all that she was pretending the apartment they were renovating was for themselves, creating a beautiful home that they designed together where they would live in bliss.

Mademoiselle Gaiman pull yourself together, she mentally admonished herself. *Tuck that attraction into the top drawer of the dresser you're repairing and never open it again.*

Nothing useful could come from these musings. Jules had given her a professional boost for which she'd forever be grateful. That was it.

"In addition to the electrician, the painters will be

at work today," he said, while looking down at some paperwork from a different project. "I'll stop by at the end of the day."

Here she'd been having such lofty thoughts about unchaining Jules's more carefree side and about tables for two, while he had his mind on his business. Still, man did not live by green drinks alone, and the recipe wasn't going to keep him healthy if he didn't have some downtime and recreation.

"Why don't we meet there at five o'clock?"

"Yes, five is good," he answered without raising his head.

"After that, what would you think about spending the rest of the afternoon doing something relaxing?" She hadn't meant to ask him that, or maybe she had?

"I don't relax." He was, once again, barely listening as he concentrated on other matters.

"Do you think maybe you should?"

"I'll put *Find Ways to Relax* on my to-do list."

"There you go! I'm sure you'll find something really rewarding if you make it a *should* not a *want to*."

"Are you being sarcastic again?"

He lifted his eyes and his stare shot point-blank right through the screen. Her heartbeat fluttered. She relived yet again that intense kiss they'd shared. What had really happened there? For all his rules and regulations, something overtook him in that moment. She couldn't stop wondering what.

Although she had no reason to, no obligation to, she felt compelled to help him unwind a little. He needed it so. She could safely do that much without too much risk to herself, couldn't she?

"What do you think? Could you shrug off your many responsibilities for a couple of hours?"

"What did you have in mind?"

"I'll show you."

When Jules met Zoe in front of the apartment, he grinned at what he saw. There she stood straddling a bicycle while holding the handlebar of a second, both with white wicker baskets in front that were decorated with artificial flowers. "I borrowed Yasmine's bike for you."

"I can see."

Zoe looked so adorable it took Jules a couple of breaths to settle into the moment. She wore a short and flowing dress made from a fabric with pink, blue and yellow flowers on it. Her hair was tied back with a pink ribbon and she wore retro-style sunglasses and a pair of flat leather sandals. She was a vision of happy, carefree Paris, even though Jules knew by now there was depth and pain beneath her cheery exterior.

He reached for one of the bike's handles and in the process their hands touched each other's. How thrilling the sensation was. After entering the building, they propped the bikes against a wall and did a quick check of the progress on the apartment.

"I haven't ridden in years," Jules confessed when they were back on the street. He held the borrowed bike, amused that he'd be riding with the girly white basket in front. While hotel concierges throughout the world had tried to encourage him to see their fair cities from a bicycle seat, Jules had always refused. He preferred his efficient morning run for his exercise. And a driver to whisk him anywhere he wanted to go.

"Bicycling through Paris, isn't that just a classic thing to do?"

"I used to bike when I was a kid." Indeed, Jules could clearly recall the exhilaration he'd had riding through the streets, pedaling as fast as he could through the outskirts of town where he lived. That was one of the few good memories he had. The wind blowing his hair back, his body leaning into turns or curves he had to maneuver. Whatever challenges the road brought were easy compared to what awaited him at home.

He adjusted the seat to accommodate his height, his fingers remembering the mechanisms of the bike as if it had been yesterday. In fact, Yasmine's bike was so basic it reminded him of a child's. None of the precision advances of sportsman bikes available today. "Where to?" he asked Zoe, aware of how rarely he'd asked that question of someone else, as it was always him making the decisions.

"Follow me."

The long list of things Jules needed to take care of flickered across his mind like news captions ticking across the bottom of the screen on television. But another part of him, one he hadn't seen in a long while, told him it was okay to let everything sit for a couple of hours. His parents were at the hotel and Karim had rescheduled a couple of meetings. The world really wouldn't come crashing down without his constant supervision.

Zoe gestured for them to turn at the intersection and again at a side street, where traffic was light and they could pick up speed.

Deciding to surrender the ride to Zoe's control, he let her stay a little bit ahead of him. Which afforded him a lovely view of her on the bike. Her petite frame was shapely. The thin fabric of the sundress billowed as she pedaled, allowing glimpses of the creamy skin of her thighs. The back of her pale neck was exposed by the ribbon that bound her hair.

Before long he was imagining his lips grazing the back of that neck underneath her hairline. He flashed back to how impossibly silky her pillowy lips were when he kissed her. How scorching and potent his tongue was with his mouth on hers. He wouldn't mind doing it again.

What if he pulled his bike up right next to hers and then at a moment when they stopped at a traffic light, he'd just lean over and touch his lips to hers? He was glad that she was a bit ahead of him so he didn't have to hide the silly grin that swept across his face at the idea.

As he was beginning to suspect, Zoe was leading him to the Luxembourg Gardens, one of the most storied and visited locales in Paris. Not only was it a must-stop for many tourists, Parisians considered it a prime spot to relax and take a break from the active and densely populated streets of the inner city.

"Let's sit by the Medici Fountain," she said as she dismounted her bike once they entered the garden gates.

"My favorite part of the gardens," he said as he gazed at Zoe. The curls that had emancipated themselves from her pink ribbon framed her face. The trail of freckles that traveled from one cheekbone across her nose to the other were fresh and natural in the late afternoon light.

"Mine, too."

They walked their bikes to the fountain with its long rectangular water basin surrounded by shady trees. A place that had been immortalized in countless paintings and photographs. Metal chairs lined each side of the basin, where people had been coming to bask for centuries. The expanse of still water gave way to the fountain with its statues and columns.

"What a nice idea to bring me here," Jules mused, swept into the beauty and peace surrounding him. Were the plane trees fragrant or was that his imagination?

"Let's sit."

They scoped out the available seating. A group of older men occupied part of the space, their chairs turned toward each other in an impromptu circle as they talked using many hand gestures. A woman read a paperback while holding her teeny dog. Schoolchildren, under the watch of a nanny, squealed and played a hopping game. It was almost a step back in time, the tableau set long ago. Jules had to admit he welcomed not being able to spot a cell phone.

He pointed to a couple of empty chairs and pulled them to the basin's edge, the scrape of the metal legs audible as he did so.

Once they sat, Zoe produced bottles of cold water from her bicycle's basket and handed him one, which was most appreciated. Popping the cap, Jules took a sip.

"Look at how much shade these trees provide," she said, noting the way the sunlight broke into shards as it danced on the basin's water.

"Perfect lighting design, right?"

"If you listen for it, you can hear the leaves rustle."

They sat in silence for a few minutes, indeed hearing the leaves' song. Jules could actually sense his heart rate slow, his breath become easy and unrestricted with deep inhales and even longer exhales. It was as if oxygen was reaching cells that had been starved of it for

ANDREA BOLTER 119

years. A pleasant tingle meandered through his blood vessels. His palms opened and tilted upward. "You were right. A person does need to do a little bit of nothing on occasion."

"This is some darn good nothing, isn't it?"

"Yes," he whispered and fell into a meditative state for a few minutes. His eyes closed. Everything fell away except a gentle wind on his face and the presence of Zoe beside him.

Eventually she said, "Our next destination will be a bit of something, though."

"Intriguing. I'm in your hands." Jules bit his lip. He hadn't meant to say something so flirty—it just slipped out. Zoe was turning him into someone he'd never met. A man he might like to know, to become. Who embraced existence on mental, physical and spiritual levels. Someone open and emancipated. A man who said yes.

After they'd thoroughly enjoyed the fountain and its surroundings, they ambled through more of the garden. Zoe led them to a café within the grounds where people sat savoring an early evening drink or snack outdoors. She chose a shady table and when the waiter approached, Zoe took the lead.

"We'll have a *tartelette des fruits*, a *fondant citron* with Chantilly *crème* and a crepe with cocoa noisette spread. Two hot chocolates and two glasses of champagne. And give the bill to him." She pointed to Jules, eliciting a belly laugh from him and a chuckle from the waiter.

"You're trying to corrupt me?" Another flirt. Not only couldn't he stop himself, he didn't want to. "You know I don't indulge in sweets."

"Exactly. On your relaxation day, you're not going to eat leaves. You're only going to look at them. Although maybe we'll have them with dinner later."

"We're having dinner?"

"If you play your cards right." She shot him a sly smile.

Zoe, he wanted to scream! *Stop saying sexy things!* Bad enough that he was thinking them. She'd already gotten him to ditch all the items on his agenda to go bike riding. And here they sat surrounded by the flora, dirt under their feet. Now she'd ordered desserts! If he didn't watch himself, Zoe might tear down the carefully guarded kingdom walls he'd created. Which, it seemed, a part of him was desperate to let her demolish.

The waiter delivered everything on a large silver tray. Zoe and Jules each put a napkin on their laps and their forks went to work.

He thought surely his eyes were going to roll back in his head at the taste of the warm crepe. He savored the thick hazelnut and chocolate flavor as it swirled around in his mouth. "Oh, my goodness."

"You've heard that expression," she said with a satisfied smile. "Life is uncertain so we should eat dessert first."

As she took a bite of the fondant Chantilly, a bit of whipped cream lingered on the side of her mouth. Jules leaned over and with a swipe of his thumb, removed the swirl from her face. And immediately, without thinking about it, licked it off. Afterward, he was a bit embarrassed at the informality.

She didn't seem bothered by it, though, and they continued peering at the gardens laid out in front of them. Vivid flowers in every shade of the rainbow surrounded the circular lawn with its statuary in front of the Luxembourg Palace.

Time passed at a leisurely pace Jules was so unaccustomed to. Every last speck on each plate was consumed and not a drop of the drinks remained. He and Zoe conversed about books and music and movies. About politics and history. The more they talked, the more he wanted to continue, speaking on any topic that came into their minds.

The moon began to rise when they decided it was time to go.

"Really, we should pick up some salads for dinner after all those sweet indulgences," she decided.

"We could bring them back to my apartment."

Jules hadn't had a guest in his Paris apartment in years, as he had used it so infrequently. He welcomed the idea. Like it was an actual home where he might have friends over. A weak voice in the back of his head tried to caution him that if he was counting, this was his third date with Zoe. And perhaps bringing her to his apartment was a bit too intimate. But his rationalizations and equations were no longer making sense to him.

Zoe gasped comically when she saw the size of Jules's apartment.

"Make yourself at home," he said casually. And then was surprised when she took him literally, unclasping her sandals and tossing them in a corner as she gave herself a self-guided tour. She took note of his upscale furniture and well-appointed office, every cord and cable to his high-tech setup discreetly out of view.

"Can I have a look at the rest?"

He'd have laughed at her lack of pretension if he weren't so charmed by it.

"Have at it, *cherie*."

She moved to the kitchen, opening cabinets and drawers. Naturally, everything was done with top-notch building materials and craftsmanship.

"Premium quartz," she mentioned as she touched his countertop.

In the master bedroom, she bounced her small hand across the foot of his oversized bed, testing the firmness of his mattress. "Is that a Leon Villar?" she asked about the abstract landscape painting above the headboard.

"It is."

"Did you see his show at Galerie Pauline Caron?"

"I saw the show in New York."

He was glad for the painting discussion as having Zoe in his bedroom was unnerving. Namely, because he couldn't stop picturing laying her down on his bed, and letting his hands, mouth and more explore all of her body that he'd not yet seen. That flimsy little dress she wore would slip over her head in one pull, and whatever was underneath he'd remove with a quick slide.

Jules's feet moved toward her. He called for that warning voice in his head but it had become so faint he really couldn't hear it. It had morphed into a distant buzz that he was easily able to shush.

Her look in response to him moving closer was affirming. Lips slightly parted, the sparkle in her eyes welcomed him.

There was only one thing to do, and so he did it. He wrapped his hand around the back of Zoe's neck and brought her face toward him as he bent down to bring the first of many kisses to her inviting mouth.

It was better than any dream he'd ever had. As Jules

delivered yet another shower of light kisses to Zoe's lovely face, each brush of his lips against her skin presented a dilemma. On one hand, he wanted to slow himself down and register each kiss before he went on to the next. But a conflicting need was ready to devour her with urgency. It was a delicious agony, choosing between the two and settling somewhere in the middle.

Just a few minutes ago, they were picking up salads from a nearby market, after their pastry-fueled sunset at the Luxembourg Gardens. Dinner in tow, they'd brought the bikes to the entrance foyer of Jules's flat. He'd have his driver return them to her apartment later. Better still, he'd also send Zoe and her roommate new bikes with all the latest innovations.

Now he was kissing her at the foot of his bed. He held his lips above hers, just close enough for her to feel his breath and want more. The hiss of her inhale emboldened him.

Both palms cupped her face. He dragged his mouth away from hers, with a tormenting pull, so that he could feather his way down to her jawline. She lifted her chin toward him, a blessing that allowed him to apply his kisses in a continuous line. The journey took him from the plump bottom of one earlobe and down one side of her face. He wasn't done until he traveled her jaw to the other side. The thrum of pleasure that elicited from somewhere low within her prompted him to discover more.

When he brought his face against the cool of her throat, his teeth bared themselves and began tiny nibbles. He reveled in her aura, breathing in her powdery sweetness. With an easy tug, he undid the ribbon that by then had been containing only half of Zoe's physics-defying orange curls. Her hair cascaded down over her shoulders, as shiny and alive as Zoe herself was.

His fingers wove through her locks—something he'd been wanting to do since he'd met her, so mesmerizing were they to him. In fact, he took pleasure from just pressing an individual curl tightly and then releasing it to watch it spring open.

"My hair is fascinating to you?" she asked after he'd performed the operation several times.

"I can't stop myself from touching it."

"Don't, then. Don't stop anything."

Their eyes met, his wearing a dark veil of arousal and hers crystalline with alertness. Jules paused with a moment of clarity. Nothing about this made sense. Why would he want to disrupt his carefully laid-out plans?

Don't stop anything.

She'd just cooed those words straight into his soul, although she might not know the extent of her effect on him. Before he could second-guess himself anymore, his hands glided down to her two shoulders. He caressed them, his fingers taking note of each of her bones and their alignment. His hands were so big they covered her shoulders completely.

He bent to kiss from the bottom of her throat down to the low neckline of her sundress. When his tongue reached the fabric, it flicked under the thin cotton. Just knowing that his mouth had met skin that the dress had been concealing stirred his very core. Her head fell back as she welcomed his exploration, which he continued with focus. His mouth took the temperature of which spots on her throat and her décolleté felt the warmest. Between her breasts was a honeyed heaven where his lips had to linger.

Eventually straightening up, he locked her in an embrace, as he suddenly needed to feel her tightly against him. Although she was petite, he found her not fragile but resilient, her body arching to meet his every move. When he molded her to him, she became pliant. Yet, she was anything but passive. Tender sighs mingled with erotic moans.

"Zoe, you're doing something to me I hadn't planned on."

"You've lit me, as well."

Filled with emotion and sensation and a primal hunger in his belly that wouldn't be contained, he pulled her down onto the bed with him. Climbing on top of her, he acknowledged how lucky his hands and lips were to be roaming over Zoe's velvety beauty. In his eagerness, he kissed her every way his body told him to. A peck on her nose. An assertive bite to the crook of her neck. The taste of the inside of her wrist.

"I haven't felt this much desire in..." Jules stopped himself before revealing what might be his best-kept secret. That he hadn't wanted someone like he wanted her. Not *in years*, which was what he had been going to say. But ever. Ever!

And it wasn't just sexual attraction he was experiencing. She'd opened his eyes to the possibility of a true connection with someone. Something that was honest and fulfilling and sustaining.

After what he witnessed as a child, he'd never trust anyone with his heart, but it was nice to know he could even have those feelings. That he was still human. Zoe showed him an alternate universe where love and beauty were everywhere. She'd changed him. He'd always be grateful for, or maybe tormented by, the gift she had given him.

"What, Jules? What are you trying to say?" Her voice sang out from the avalanche of kisses he was bestowing on her.

"Only that… I'm glad you're here." With that, his mouth found hers again where their tongues met for an extended swirl that pulled Jules into an ocean's tide. His hand began a journey along her thigh, slipping under her dress.

When he leaned his neck back, the passion he saw in her eyes must have been a mirror. He swept Zoe's flowery little dress up over her head and tossed it on the chair beside his bed.

CHAPTER SEVEN

ZOE COULD HARDLY believe she was being seduced by, and for that matter seducing, Jules. She told herself she'd better enjoy this unbelievable moment in time because it would be gone in a flash and was unlikely to ever happen again.

You're doing something to me I hadn't planned on.

His words were spoken in the heat of desire. She had the good sense to not take them seriously. Still, she was a sophisticated denizen of Paris who was free to indulge in a night of impassioned intimacy with an extraordinary man.

So, with the ever-present eye of the Eiffel Tower visible through the window of Jules's bedroom, Zoe pulled him tight, her warning ping screaming from within. She'd never been with a man like him. The few boyfriends she'd had back in Maupont were of adult age but they were still boys, fumbling and tentative, unsure of themselves. Jules was 100 percent man. His power and command as an executive was matched by the strength and confidence emanating from him as a lover.

After he'd taken off every stitch of clothing she wore, he quickly undid the buttons of his shirt and cast it off to the side, as well. Then he was on top of her again, his weight melding her into his bed. She wrapped her arms around his shoulders, his lean muscles defined underneath warm smooth skin.

His hands moved down her outline and then underneath her to bring her body up even closer to him as he pressed his still-clad maleness against her bare and now pulsating center. There they kissed and swayed, embarking toward a destination they didn't yet see.

When craving demanded more, Zoe reached between them to unbuckle Jules's belt and unzip the fly of his pants. Excited by the fullness that she stroked with her palm, her other hand yanked at his remaining clothes. With a devilish grin, he backed away from her to peel off his trousers. He reached for a condom in his nightstand and unrolled it before returning to her arms where their bodies finally truly joined and became one.

Zoe gripped him, wrapped her legs around his waist, as they flew up to the heavens, now knowing where they were going. They ascended higher and higher and higher still until, together, they soared freely as one.

When they landed back down, he collapsed on top of her. Her fingers combed through his hair with a sense of possessiveness, like he belonged to her. It was a heady sensation. Her every breath oozed an earthy, womanly sensuality she'd never known in herself.

After a serene interval of recuperation, Jules announced, "I want to eat."

"We still have our salads."

He separated himself from her, which, at first, was a torturous desertion. It had only been to gather up a few items of clothing. He stepped back into his boxers and black slacks, though he left the top button open, pulled his belt from the pant loops and cast that aside. Zoe slipped on her dress and undies, leaving her bra where it sat on Jules's side chair. He reached for her hand and led her, barefoot, into the kitchen.

As he sat her down at his chrome bar table with its two stools facing each other, Zoe wondered how many women had occupied the second seat at his table, literally or figuratively throughout his world travels.

"Have you ever lived with anyone?" she asked as Jules opened the fridge.

He lashed his head toward her in a way that made Zoe apprehensive that she'd angered him with her inquisitiveness. Instead, the look in his eyes was glassy and sad, especially shadowed by the bluish light coming from inside the refrigerator. "No. I told you. That life is not for me."

Something in his face and the way his response sounded like a question melted Zoe's heart. This man was as precious as the monuments of Paris he so revered. He deserved to be happy, to be able to count on someone. He was worthy of love. How tragic it was that his past was robbing him of a future. Although the same could be said of her.

She studied the movement in the taut muscles of his back as he reached for the salads. Her body went liquid again at the sight, a reminder of what had just transpired in his bed. He flicked on some under-cabinet lighting that gave the whole room a gentle glow, nice for the late hour. After placing the food and cold drinks on the table, he perched at the stool opposite her.

They ate in quiet for an interlude. Zoe's body was still lost in his embrace but her mind had gone to thought. When a little too much time passed, it became oppressive. She believed him when he said that he didn't get close to people and would never couple with anyone. Making love with her had not changed that one iota. Why would it? It wasn't as if she was used to a scenario like this, either. She'd come to Paris to make a career for herself, hopefully to have interesting friends and a full life. Since she'd been here, she hadn't been in a man's bed nor shared hers.

After keeping his eyes on his salad, the awkwardness got to Jules as well and he flicked a remote control on the table to turn on the television. They watched the news together, although she wasn't paying attention to the words coming out of the anchorman's mouth—something about roadwork in the Eighteenth Arrondissement.

There was no denying that an overwhelming yearning had been satiated between them in Jules's bedroom. They fit perfectly together in that respect, as if their bodies were meant for each other's. Only for each other's. But something passed between their hearts as well, something poignant, life-altering. She couldn't have been the only one to have felt it. Although, she had the sense that tomorrow she'd need to figure out how to put all of that to the side and move on with their professional interactions. Jules had made his intentions, or lack thereof, clear from the beginning.

Perhaps they were the cliché of those European types who casually mixed business with pleasure? If so, she should be able to laugh this off, just one night of many free-flowing encounters. After the ecstasy Jules brought her, the heights of giving and receiving pleasure that were new to her, to turn to a self-conscious kitchen snack in the dead of night did not come naturally to her. In fact, for reasons she couldn't coalesce into one explanation, she was fighting back tears.

But it was time to pretend that they didn't care about each other. That's how these nonchalant affairs went. Chitchat was in order and luckily Jules provided. "I'm concerned the two wing-backed chairs for the bedroom are too big in scale." He was referring to the furniture delivery for the apartment that had arrived earlier today. Before the bike ride and the Luxembourg Gardens and her tongue tracing down his spine.

"I'll look at it again with fresh eyes tomorrow," she answered in a scratchy late-night voice, determined to keep up. "It's true that they're more decorative than anything else since it wouldn't be worth the trouble for your father to get out of his wheelchair to sit in them. I'd like to fill in that space, though."

"I still like the idea of a bench. The depth would be so much shorter."

That conversation petered out and they went back to watching the news.

"Well, it's late and I'd like to get some sleep," Jules said after they finished eating.

Did he mean that he wanted *them* to get some sleep or that he wanted her to leave? Again, Zoe racked her brain, trying to figure out how worldly adults who have had sex but aren't together handle these situations. No wonder she didn't do blasé encounters. It was too confusing.

"I… I should be going, then," she managed, figuring that was the safest thing to say.

"You're welcome to stay…" His voice was unconvincing and he cast his eyelids downward. He was feeling as uneasy as she was, so different from the master-of-the-universe persona he usually projected to the world.

On one hand, she wanted to hold him all night long, perhaps including more of the divine lovemaking they had created and then nestling herself into him as they fell into one dream. On the other, she couldn't get away fast enough, to provide herself with a shield before any more affection toward him would promise inevitable disappointment. Being wise, or so she thought, she chose the latter.

After returning from collecting her things in the bedroom, she slipped on her shoes. "Are we still going to see your apartment on the Grands Boulevards later this week?"

"Yes." He tapped on his phone. "I've just called a driver to take you home. Let me walk you down."

At the late hour, Paris was subdued outside of Jules's building but still awake. Some young people laughed loudly as they passed by. A few cars and motorbikes tooled down the boulevard. When the driver pulled to the curb, Jules opened the door and helped Zoe into the back seat. He leaned in to give her a kiss good-night that belied their parting. It was a kiss that informed them, in case they hadn't figured it out yet, that they'd entered the danger zone. Their feelings for each other were anything but meaningless.

"I'll need a phone conference with Kowalczyk and his contractor today," Jules instructed Karim as they walked out of a meeting at Durand headquarters that had his head spinning. "If he doesn't get his materials cost under control, I'm pulling out."

"I let his people know."

"Run me a comparison sheet on what he'd budgeted versus what his estimates are now."

"Yes, Jules."

"And call our legal team and find out what my obligations are at this point."

"I will do that." Karim spoke in a calm monotone that Jules appreciated. Jules would be spending more time in person with his assistant now that he'd be based in Paris. The thought didn't displease him.

"Get the architect on the phone," Jules instructed as he rounded the corner to his office while Karim continued forward.

Entering his office, Jules tossed the file he was holding onto his desk, shrugged off his jacket and loosened his tie. Mounting his treadmill, he set it for a slow walk to help him blow off some steam.

With the city laid out in front of him, he realized that he was overreacting to the work setback. He'd dealt with developers who went over budget many times. His agitation didn't have that much to do with Krakow.

What was bothering him was how uncomfortably things had ended with Zoe last night after they'd made love. It had been so authentic and uncomplicated, spending that time with her at the Luxembourg Gardens and then at his apartment. Like a dance that he already knew the steps to, being with her came easily. He hadn't needed to strategically fortress himself with walls to keep out emotions. Although, maybe he subconsciously had in the end. Because after all the surprising naturalness of them getting out of bed together to eat a late supper in the kitchen, Jules stepped out of himself and saw the situation like someone looking in. And in that instant, the realness he felt turned itself fake in his stomach like rotten food. And he had to get away from it as quickly as he could.

Tucking a woman into a waiting car in the middle of the night. Three-date rules. A vow never to marry. Jules Durand had become the man he'd set out to be. Only now it was someone he didn't like.

"Hello," Jules said with a quick kiss to her cheek when he met Zoe in front of one of his buildings a few days later as planned. Most of the decisions on the apartment for his parents had been made but he'd promised to take her to one of his most show-stopping properties.

He seemed cheerier than he had when they'd parted in the wee hours that night after they'd made love, with her peering out the back-seat window at him as the driver pulled the car away, distress washing over Jules's exquisite face.

"You own this?" she asked, even though the answer was obvious. "The entire building?"

"1869. Haussmann."

Georges-Eugène Haussmann, the prefect under Emperor Napoléon III who redesigned a decaying city into the metropolis and crossroads Paris remained to this day. Haussmann demolished the medieval city neighborhoods that were unhealthy, overcrowded and dangerous, and replaced them with a new Paris. Enormous apartment buildings were built, not to be considered as individual structures but as part of an urban landscape with wide avenues and public squares. That signature architectural style became the look of Paris, the front-facing windows and horizontal designs of similar heights, building-front after building-front cut from cream-colored stone.

Zoe's mind boggled that Jules owned one of those buildings, and at what price it might fetch on the modern market. She shook her head. "I know I'm a small-town girl but it's hard to believe I actually know someone who owns a Haussmann on the Grands Boulevards of Paris."

Jules's mouth twitched. She could tell he wasn't actually smiling at her lack of savvy, only that she'd voiced it out loud. "All right, Mademoiselle Small Town, my property manager arranged for us to see one of the apartments in the building. From what I'm told, my tenant uses a wheelchair and we've made some excellent accommodations for her I'd like to show you."

"Wonderful. Lead the way." Zoe pointed to the entrance door.

So far, so good, she noted of the easier rapport they were managing today. Although, entering the building, she moved close to him and it was all she could do not to lean in. To beg those strong shoulders to encircle her, a return to the magical private universe they'd escaped to in his bed.

All business, Jules used his passcode to enter the apartment.

"Wow," Zoe exclaimed. "Did we just walk into the Palais Versailles? I've never seen anything like this." It appeared that every wall that was not part of the building's intrinsic structure had been removed, artistic pillars concealing foundational beams that were necessary to retain. In doing so, a vast expanse had been created, almost beyond what the eye could see. "I can't believe this is a center-city residence."

"By taking out as many walls as we could, we've

made it easier for Madame to maneuver around the apartment."

"Less doorways and corners. Not to mention the majesty of it all."

"I'm very pleased with how this turned out. And when Madame decides to move out, I'm sure many tenants would appreciate this open plan."

"Ya!" Zoe shrieked, getting a giggle out of Jules. "This has to be the best apartment in Paris. The Grands Boulevards are my favorite part of the city, anyway."

"Come here." He took her hand and brought her to the farthest windows where there was a clear view of the opera house, Palais Garnier.

"Did you know that the opera house was once the nexus of Paris's high society?" she asked.

"What operas have you seen at the Palais?"

"None. I've never been."

"You've never gone to the opera in Paris?"

"I've never been to an opera anywhere."

"We'll have to correct that immediately. Do you have plans tonight?" He didn't wait for an answer as he pulled his phone from his jacket pocket. "Karim, get me an opera box for tonight."

Zoe heart rate sped. Jules was calling his assistant to get opera tickets for them? Just like that?

After the strangeness at his apartment, she hadn't known what to expect today. She'd been working on his parents' apartment independently while Jules was dealing with other properties. She'd updated him during FaceTime sessions but the uneasiness between them had still hung in the air. It was a relief that he was less quirky today.

"I thought you didn't make spur-of-the-moment decisions," she chided him, giddy energy propelling her to make a joke.

"I must be spending too much time with you." He grinned back. "Do you have anything to wear?"

"Can I wear the orange dress you bought me for that cruise on the Seine?"

"You could. But let's buy you something new."

She shrugged her shoulders. "Whatever you say, boss." The quip earned her another chortle from Jules. Their jokey manner was keeping them from dealing with the reality of their night together, both the incendiary lovemaking and the prickly aftermath. But if he wanted to play it that way, so would she. Maybe they could find an equilibrium. In any case, she was going to the opera.

"We may as well go to Galeries Lafayette." Paris's most famous and sophisticated department stores were conveniently located nearby. Jules tapped into his phone again. "Karim, I also need a personal shopper at Galeries Lafayette right away."

After touring the rest of the apartment, they walked the few blocks to the store and entered into its massive sales floor. Each of the store's upper levels, which were flanked with archways, were visible from the center of the ground floor. That drew the eye upward to the styling of the art nouveau multi-colored steel and glass dome. It was another architectural masterpiece. Zoe marveled, "This store is a museum piece in and of itself."

An elevator took them to their floor and they were shown into a sequestered salon. The overstuffed furniture was upholstered in a baby pink and the carpet a pretty caramel. A dais surrounded by mirrors anchored the space.

A young saleswoman introduced herself as Safa. She wore a navy sheath dress with a multi-colored scarf tied around her neck just so, the knot at one side where it magically stayed in place. "I understand you'd like something special for the opera?"

"We would." Jules nodded.

"Did you have something in mind?"

Jules turned to Zoe. "What would be your fantasy opera outfit? I'll wear a tuxedo."

"Old-fashioned romance, I guess. Is black velvet okay?" she questioned. After all, Jules was paying for another dress. She expected he'd want to approve it as he had last time.

"If that's what you'd like."

"I'll be back with some suggestions," Safa said and then exited the salon.

When Jules arrived at Zoe's apartment that night to pick her up for the opera, Yasmine was home, as well. "Ni... ice to meet you," she stammered. Zoe couldn't blame her, as Jules's mere presence seemed to overtake their tiny apartment. It was as if all of the furniture moved out of the way to allow his entrance.

With his substantial height and precision haircut, his slim-cut black tux gave him that look of modern royalty. Every inch of him was faultlessly chic, from the jacket's thin lapel to his luxury wristwatch to his shoes on which a scuff would never dare appear. It was almost comical the way Yasmine's eyes all but bugged out like a cartoon character.

But when Zoe stepped into Jules's view in her ensemble, it was she who drew the approving gaze. As a matter of fact, he cleared his throat in response, which Zoe found adorable. "You look spectacular," he said.

No one had ever called her that before and she almost blushed. Memories of making love with him flooded her. The way his body, his fingers, his mouth had appreciated her and made her feel *spectacular*. Her heart sat heavy with the knowledge that she might never share that glory with him again. Even if she had the opportunity, she'd have to turn it down. Her emotions had already grown perilous. Nonetheless, one of Paris's most attractive bachelors was taking her to the opera, and she was going to turn her mind to savoring every moment of the fairy-tale evening.

So, she quite enjoyed the lustful way he looked her over from top to bottom. He, of course, had sent a stylist to the apartment to help her get dressed, and her unruly hair had been corralled but left curly in a half-up, half-down do. Her smoky eye makeup was dramatic and the most perfect shade of pale lipstick complemented her complexion.

Zoe absolutely loved the dress she'd picked out from the choices the saleswoman at Galeries Lafayette had brought them earlier. Crushed velvet, it had a wide and low-cut neckline. So jet-black it was almost blue. The shapewear undergarment she wore enhanced her bosom, displaying as much voluptuousness as was tasteful. The dress fit her like a glove, hugging all her curves until it reached a lower calf hemline that was flattering on her. And the nude heels gave it a freshness that the more customary black shoe wouldn't have.

"I think there's something missing," Jules stated after his long gander. He stepped closer to her as he removed a midnight blue jewelry box from his jacket pocket. Flipping it open, large diamond stud earrings sparkled from their satin berth. "These are for you."

Yasmine gasped so loudly that both Jules and Zoe snapped their heads toward her. He smiled at her roommate's zest. Jules took one of the earrings from the box and removed its backing. "May I?"

"Yes!" Yasmine blurted. The three of them giggled. With, mysteriously, the knowledge of how to fit earrings onto a woman, Jules graced her lobe with the heavy jewel. His thick fingers understood the task, gently sliding the post in and then affixing the back. The whole process was so profoundly erotic Zoe's eyelashes fluttered and beads of sweat began to form between her breasts. Then he repeated his ministrations with her other ear. She tried to calm herself with slow breaths but to no avail. She was no match for this man's charms.

Pleased with his handiwork Jules decreed, "Perfect."

And divine everything was, as his driver delivered them to the Palais Garnier, one of Paris's most famous addresses for centuries. The ornate building's exterior was decorated at every inch with statues, columns, friezes and sculpture done in stones and metals. It wasn't hard to see why ghostly lore and novels such as *The Phantom of the Opera* were set in amongst such splendor.

Jules escorted her inside and when they reached the Grand Staircase, Zoe could hardly believe she was there. The swooping double staircases crafted of fine marble led up to either side of the foyer. They were even more magnificent in their detail than she had seen in photos and paintings.

"You know, part of the reason these staircases were designed to curve as they do was so that people could get a clear view of who was here and what they wore," she said. "This used to be *the* place for gossip and scandal."

"You've read up, I see."

He crooked his arm to begin leading her up those lavish marble stairs. "Careful with those high heels—" he winked "—we don't want you falling into the opera like you fell into my office. Modern-day scandal as Paris mogul takes adorable klutz to *Madame Butterfly.*"

"You're never going to let me live that down, are you?"

"Not a chance."

She scrunched her face but he knew that she appreciated his humor. Still, she took hold of one of the elaborate balustrades and kept her other arm in Jules's. Feeling quite splendid, she reached the top of the stairs, secretly grateful to do it without bobbling.

"My gosh," she exclaimed as they took their seats in the box he'd reserved. The sumptuous horseshoe-shaped auditorium was rich with its red and gold decor. A bronze and crystal chandelier led to the ceiling painting done by Marc Chagall. "I'd read about this Chagall ceiling. I've forgotten when was it done?"

"In the 1960s."

"I think what I was reading said they installed it over the ceiling's original artwork."

"Another example of the old and the new merging in Paris."

When the lights were lowered for the opera to begin, Zoe's stomach twisted. The moment, the splendor of the opera house and her enchantment with Jules should have been perfect. Yet, the extreme discomfort the night after they'd made love still twirled within her like a ballerina's pirouette. She hoped her inner pinging would quiet down enough for her to enjoy the performance.

And Puccini's beauty and poignancy did captivate her attention. She sat motionless and spellbound for the entire first act.

At the first intermission, Jules suggested they visit the Grand Foyer, the long gilded hall with crystal, gold leaf and ceiling paintings that seemed to stretch the length of a city block. The social scene in the Paris of years gone by had gathered in this hallowed expanse, apparently sometimes several nights a week. Zoe could see why. It was opulence rarely seen outside of a palace. Zoe imagined women in the elaborate dresses of centuries past, corsets and gold braiding, tiny shoes with buckles and powdery wigs. Or, later, women with red lipstick and their short hair tucked into cloche hats. The foyer was a history lesson come to life.

"I want to show you something," Jules said as he took her hand. She wasn't able to hide the jolt that his firm grasp produced in her. He took her out to the loggia, the large span of balcony where the night air invigorated Zoe's face.

Tears pooled in her eyes at the sight of everything. The loggia overlooked the Place de l'Opéra, the open public square and the wide boulevards of what was called the Haussmann-Opéra neighborhood. Just as rideshares and scooters now moved people to and fro, she could picture the same streets filled with horses and carriages. Times were different but, in a way, Paris had stayed the same. That was why she'd moved here. To be part of the past and the future of this inimitable city.

"Jules, thank you for tonight. For bringing me here."

"I need to tell you something." He turned his face to

her as they stood in front of the view. "I want to apologize for the other night. I shouldn't have let you leave like that. As I've told you, I don't enter into romantic attachments. My attraction to you got carried away and then after our beautiful lovemaking interlude I...panicked I suppose is the right word."

She girded herself. Here would come the words she was expecting, the words that she knew were in both of their interests. He'd say definitively, lest there be any confusion, that what happened between them was impulsive and that he doesn't *do* impulsive. That they should just chock it up to a mistake, which would never occur again. Just as their original kiss had been.

It really would be for the best. She'd shake her head in agreement. Neither of them were open to falling in love. There was no benefit to continuing a personal acquaintance. They were colleagues and nothing more.

Take a mental snapshot, Zoe.

Because this was all she was getting. This night, this loggia, this stunning and affecting man. She'd cherish and replay all of it until her dying day.

"And?" She encouraged him to finish, wanting her pain served up quickly like a bandage being ripped from delicate skin.

"And..." He lingered before leaning down to take hold of her face and give her a profoundly sensual kiss that snaked all the way down into her belly, coiling in her very soul. "And I want a do-over. I want you in my bed again. And this time I want to hold you all night."

After they returned to their box seats, the tragic longing of Cio-Cio San's famous second-act aria paled in comparison to the music in Zoe's heart.

CHAPTER EIGHT

JULES PLACED A wisp of a kiss on the head of a still-sleeping Zoe in his bed. He grabbed some running gear from a drawer and padded quietly out of the room, not wanting to wake her. After he dressed for his early-morning exercise, he opened the fridge to make sure the green smoothies were there. He and Zoe would have those for breakfast when he returned.

On the street, cafés were open to meet the needs of those already out and about. Shop owners pulled back their safety gates, fishmongers stacked the latest catches on ice. Jules ran past a fruit vendor, the proprietor in a white apron inspecting his offerings, pulling off apples that he deemed unsellable and tossing them into a box under his display stand. Neon lights in a supermarket window looked eerie in the still-sleepy morning, but customers entered and exited. The optometry office, the bank and the pet groomers were not yet open.

Traffic chugged along but few horns honked. In the hum of daybreak, Jules could think. Before demands yanked his concentration from one thing to another to another still. That Krakow project still had him worried. He was missing some information and he'd need to schedule a teleconference as soon as he got to the office.

He increased his running pace. And would his parents be able to make a new chapter of their lives here? Could they manage to set aside their differences, at least some of the time, to grow old together with any amount of grace and respect? Nothing in their past suggested that they would but out of sheer will Jules was hoping against hope that he could create some kind of unit between the three of them that had never existed in the first place.

At the moment, though, he didn't want to think about their issues any more than he did those in Krakow. There was only one thing he wanted on his mind.

Zoe. Charming, vivacious, warm-hearted Zoe. With whom he'd spent a night that alternated from sweet affection to savage hunger. That left them sweating and panting to the point that they could hear each other's breath afterward as they lay spent on his bed. And instead of being satisfied, Jules wanted more.

He ran past his local boulangerie and got a whiff of the yeasty baked goods he was able to see through the shop's open street-facing window.

After he had kissed Zoe so passionately on the loggia of the opera house and stated that he wanted her to come home with him, he waited in a haze of awareness for the rest of the performance, his body flinching and flexing, desperate to be free of his tuxedo. It was an exquisite torment. Their night at his apartment afterward was well worth the wait.

Reflecting on all of it as he ran, oxygen surging through him, one fact caught him by surprise. If one was to be counting, taking Zoe to the opera had been date number four. He'd disregarded his longstanding promise to himself never to go past three dates with a woman.

At the beginning, he'd rationalized that Zoe was a colleague so his tallies didn't even count. Now, he no longer cared. Maybe everything in his world could come together as one big messy whole. Once he stabilized his parents, finally stopped the commotion that he'd been running from his entire life, he'd allow in some joy. And romance. Was anything about that plan realistic, or was he being as silly as a teenager with a crush?

The existence he'd been leading had to change. It wasn't normal, wasn't healthy. When he moved aside the clutter in his brain, he knew that. A man could become nothing but a hard shell living alone, communicating only superficially to his parents or regarding business. His hot red blood would drain, his juices would dry up, the vital force of his solar plexus would shrivel.

Suddenly, while he was running and observing the life on the street around him, it was as if he could see with a bright clarity that had long been hidden. What made existence worthwhile was to spend it amongst other people. Having a shared experience. The ups. The downs. The maybes. Caring and being cared for. And it was Zoe who had opened his eyes.

On a whim, he circled back and started running in the direction he came from. With a ridiculous amount of excitement, he entered the boulangerie whose smells had tickled his nose when he'd run past earlier. The green smoothies could wait. Jules ordered two cafés au lait and four croissants, which were still warm in the bag the cashier presented.

When he got home, he went straight to the bathroom and started pouring a bath in his enormous Carrara marble tub. In his bedroom, he found Zoe just waking, stretching her sinewy arms above her head.

"Good morning."

"You've been out?" she cooed, her voice still subdued from sleep.

"My run."

"Mmm…how ambitious."

"Early bird and all that. Would you join me in a bath?"

"A morning bath, how luxurious. Do you do that every day?"

"Never."

A shy smile crossed her lips and Jules's heart twanged.

He fetched her a toothbrush and gave her a few moments of privacy in the vanity portion of his bathroom suite. Meanwhile, he found some bubble bath his housekeeper must have bought for him and yelled through the door, "Gardenia or citrus?"

"Citrus."

Once she emerged, he helped her step into the bathtub made to comfortably fit two.

"Ah…" she whooshed as she immersed herself in the fragrant bubbles.

Jules lowered himself in, as well.

He positioned them just as he had planned in his mind as he carried the coffee and croissants back after his purchase. With him leaning back against the tub's marble, he pulled Zoe between his legs so that her back rested against his chest and he could be a human pillow for her.

"I can't believe you can see the Eiffel Tower even from your bathtub," she remarked on the view through the picture window that was strategically positioned to afford total privacy. "I'd never get anything done if I had a bathroom like this."

Jules couldn't argue. With the oversized glass shower that had several faucets and jet options, plus the extra-large tub with a whirlpool motor, this room was a special oasis. Connected to the bath and shower suite was a separate water closet, double sinks in cabinets with lots of storage and a dressing table with a lighted mirror. He'd owned this apartment for years but hadn't lived in it for more than weeks at a time. Now that he thought about it, this was probably a woman's dream come true of a bathroom. A measure of his isolation was that he'd never noticed before.

"It does promote relaxation."

"Kudos to your designer on this one."

Jules couldn't remember who had done the renovations on this apartment. He'd been out of the country at the time.

"I've never taken a bath here."

"What? Why?"

"It never occurred to me." He kissed the top of Zoe's shoulder, her skin slick with soapy water. "Until this morning." Wrapping her in his long arms, he fully enveloped her and held her as close to him as was humanly possible.

The bubbles danced beautifully across her bent knees. Lucky bubbles. He kissed the top of her head over and over.

This freeze frame in time was very appealing. It was as if all at once during his run, he *got it*. That the benefits of sharing a bath, a life were well worth any sacrifices of control. His intellectual self knew that most partners didn't walk out on the other and then come crawling back, begging for forgiveness over and over again. None of what Jules grew up in was normal. In a flash, he believed for the first time that history did not have to repeat itself.

A kind of delight came over him, like nothing he'd ever felt before. Sure, there was a rush when a project was completed or an attractive property was acquired. Yet, what he experienced this morning was something different. Better. It was pure and simple optimism.

Almost unwilling to let go of Zoe for even a minute, he leaned over to the tub's ledge and handed her one of the coffees he'd bought.

"Mmm," she sighed after a sip. "Delicious."

"Like you." He dried his hands on a nearby towel so he could open the bag of croissants. Breaking off a piece, he reached his hand in front of her so that he could feed her a bite.

"Croissants for breakfast? I thought you started the day with handfuls of lawn grass or some such."

Jules laughed, his bellows echoing throughout the bathroom. "It was a spur-of-the-moment decision."

"I approve." When he fed her more, she held onto his hand so that she could take the second bite more sensually, her tongue flicking the tips of his fingers.

Their soak was about to take an entirely different turn when Jules's phone buzzed from the bedroom. Because early morning had slid, albeit lusciously, into business hours he felt he should take it.

"I'll be right back."

"Sure. But give me the rest of the croissant first."

Another chuckle made him wonder who he was. Had he learned the meaning of the word *fun*, after all?

He hoisted himself out of the bath, wrapped a towel

around his waist and went to his nightstand to retrieve his phone. His mother's voice tampered the elation that Zoe and bubbles had given him.

"I'm at the Gare du Nord." The train station. Dread thudded in the center of Jules's chest. "I am not wasting one more moment of my life on that louse you call a father. I'm leaving and this time I am truly never coming back. I'll need some money and I'll be in touch with where you should wire it."

"Mother. Stop this nonsense. Do not get on that train. I'll send a car for you. We're not doing this anymore."

"All aboard!" Jules could hear the loudspeaker in the distance.

"Mother!"

"I'm boarding now. Goodbye, son."

Lounging in the bath until her skin was pink and shriveled, Zoe followed Jules's instruction to linger as long as she wanted. As to what was so urgent based on the phone call he'd received, he merely said that he had to go and that it couldn't wait. He'd quickly donned full business garb and his serious face. Zoe assumed it had something to do with the projects he'd mentioned were running over budget. The succulent kisses goodbye he gave her didn't need any explanation.

Zoe could get used to bathing in a huge marble tub with a view. The lazy sunlight shining on the Paris rooftops made the tableau look like a painting. She oozed into some steamy daydreams of her and Jules and bubbles, his big hands making sure every spot on her body was properly soaped. Every. Spot. Those same hands that surely knew what they were doing to her on dry land last night. After the opera and the exchange on the loggia, when he begged her to understand that he'd panicked after they'd made love the first time but that he was sure he wanted her in his bed all night long. She slid underneath the water and allowed the warm cocoon to surround her.

Then, only after she'd eaten every flake of the croissants Jules had surprised her with after his run, she finally got out of the tub and used a thick fluffy towel to dry herself off. With just her black velvet dress from the night before to put on, she quickly left Jules's apartment for her own where she could change into daytime clothes.

Her next stop was Si Wu's studio to approve the living room furniture before having it delivered. Si had previously come to the apartment and, along with Jules, they'd worked out the furniture order there. It was a symbol of respect for Jules that the renowned furniture-maker had paid him a house call. Now, at his studio, Zoe appreciated roaming around his showroom, eyeing the sophisticated yet contemporary pieces Si was famous for.

Since her roommate, Yasmine, worked here, she had a chance to say hi. Yasmine came down from the stepladder she was on, having reached for something. "Didn't hear you come home last night, roomie."

All Zoe did was nod back, a smile breaking across her face.

"Zoe, hi, come, let me show you where we're at," Si cut in. He was a high-strung man with black-rimmed eyeglasses who talked and walked very fast, darting across his large studio. Zoe hustled to keep up with him. Si pointed to the rust-colored button-tufted corner piece that had sofa seating on one side and an L-shaped chaise lounge on the other. He rattled off in his rapid-fire manner of speaking. "I can add another module if you decide you want it larger, button-tufted is always so sharp looking, and wears well, what do you think?"

She inspected the creation and thought about it, picturing it in the place she'd chosen. The fine craftsmanship was evident in every facet. It was a gorgeous piece that would anchor the room. But she did have a question. "As you know, one of the occupants uses a wheelchair." Jules hadn't specifically asked her not to mention that the apartment was for his parents when they started working with Si, but she didn't think it was anyone's business. "Does it have to be so low to the ground? I'd like the tenant to be easily able to get in and out."

"I can do some custom legs to give you a little more height. You don't want to end up with a bed sort of look, especially for the chaise section, unless you do?"

Zoe was almost giddy to be having this conversation with the famous furniture designer, even if he did have an odd way of speaking. This is what she'd dreamt of. Customizing fine pieces, which, together, became a home with personality. There were no price tags on Si's furniture, unlike the showroom of her family's store in Maupont where customers needed that information. At a studio like this, a person couldn't afford his designs if they needed to ask the price.

"The dining table and chairs, end tables, side chairs, bench for the bedroom, nightstands, bed frame, daybed for second bedroom, window table, all being delivered today," Si rattled off the inventory from memory. "Is that okay with you, Zoe?"

That she was here was all because of Jules. Despite her less than graceful entry into his life, he took a chance on her. In more ways than one. She bit her lip, recalling the sensuality they'd shared last night, tuning into each other's pleasure, giving and taking, and bringing the other to ecstasy. With Jules, both professionally and personally, she felt confident and mature. Maybe her inner tide had finally turned.

"What happened *this* time?" Jules barreled into the hotel penthouse where, earlier in the week, he thought things had been a bit calmer with his parents.

"Your mother is up to her old tricks," Hugo said as he wheeled himself closer to his son and then made a dismissive wave with his hand. "It was somehow my fault that the toast got cold and then she was off and running on her tirade. I never provided enough for her. We're reduced to taking marching orders from our son who is locking us into an apartment so we can rot. Her life has been meaningless."

"To which you replied?"

"She's right. With no one to blame but herself."

"Lovely."

"This time she swears she's going to stay away until she dies so she never has to look at my sour face again. Direct quote. Reminds me of the old days."

Jules's brow furrowed, annoyed at his mother's harsh words and at having to endure his parents' theatrics yet again. While her behavior hadn't been better, at least Agathe hadn't been running away from her family the past few years. Whatever the mental process was that triggered her need to escape, with the help of Jules's money, she'd been dragging Hugo along with her. But now her old habits had reared up again, skyrocketing Jules's emotions right back to the old days.

It seemed perfectly fitting that because he'd let Durand Properties make it for half the morning without him, something he so seldom did, and he was getting genuine pleasure from a bubble bath and buttery Parisian pastries with Zoe, that his parents would ruin it for him.

"We'll have to get a nurse in to help you for the time being," Jules voiced as his mind began to spin.

"Don't be ridiculous," Hugo protested. "I don't need looking after like an invalid."

But Jules was already firing off a text to Karim to contact an agency that could find someone suitable. Taking swift action to solve a problem without any sort of debate was what had kept him from falling apart as a child, as a teenager and as an adult. It was his salvation.

No amount of order could make things right with Zoe, though. All the realizations he thought he'd come to this morning quickly burned up in smoke as if they were tossed into a bonfire. What on earth had he been thinking? That happy-in-spite-of-everything nonsense he'd begun believing was just an escape. No one, no woman he'd ever met, not even Zoe, could convince him that partnering with someone wouldn't lead to disappointment, betrayal and despair.

It was pure poppycock that humans were made to share their place in the world with someone. Quite the opposite. The safer a distance a man kept from others and their distortions, the more likely he was to fully develop himself, to find his own way and not be swayed by the needs and limitations of someone else.

Jules saw himself in his father's sneering face. They were survivors, by whatever means necessary. That much they shared in common regardless of their opposite paths. Hugo chose to be alone within a marriage. Jules wouldn't even go that far. Neither should waste time and energy dwelling on how things might be better.

Agathe must have panicked. He'd overestimated her ability to appreciate the stability he was offering. Stronger measures were necessary. For their safety. Jules was the responsible party. He couldn't take a chance that his mother would wander off without him knowing her whereabouts. He would bring in a social worker to administrate and supervise physical and mental evaluations. Bring in round-the-clock care if that's what was called for. Their situation was too much for him to manage on his own. Just like with his properties, he needed a professional team. Organization and logic would prevail, as they always had.

For now, it would be simple enough to get his mother to return this time because, without money, she wouldn't last long even if she did impose herself on some distant cousin for a few days like she used to. After that, he'd bring in a squad.

Jules knew what else he needed to do.

After he'd heard through his mother's phone the train conductor calling passengers for boarding, the desperation in Agathe's voice took Jules back to his childhood. Memories marched along his brain like ticker tape. He replayed all his mother's departure walks down the street outside of their apartment building. How young Jules would stick his head out the window to watch her. He'd rest his arms on the rotted wood of the windowsill that always left scratches on his arms. Agathe's dress or coat might be different from one season to the next, but there was always the olive-colored suitcase.

The rattle of its wheels on the sidewalk was a sound he would never forget.

Before Agathe's call, for a fleeting moment in the bathtub with Zoe, he'd supposed that he could let go of all of that. Convinced Zoe's optimism had changed him. But it turns out, that was as temporary as the bath bubbles that had coated her luscious body.

Because Agathe leaving again had emotionally exhausted him. It was the last straw. He needed to put his armor back on. He wasn't capable of such a big shift as what being with Zoe would bring. It was too late for him. He was actually fragile. Feelings had no place in his world. Shutting down was the only way he could exist. That was what he knew, his lifeline, and he couldn't surrender it. That part of him had to be selfish. The wise part, the overseer, couldn't let him pile on any more disappointment. He was done. What if he put his trust in Zoe and she left him? He wouldn't survive the loss.

Or what if he was the one to leave? After all, as much as he could intellectualize about what had happened to him as a child, it was a fact that history sometimes did repeat itself. Despite his best intentions, maybe he wouldn't be able to go the distance in a long-term relationship with her. He couldn't bear the idea of her hearing *his* suitcase teeter away. Of her poking her head out the window to watch him desert her. He couldn't bear the hurt that his leaving her would cause. He'd had no example on how to do relationships right. Certainly, he'd get it wrong. He loved Zoe too much to take a chance on breaking her heart.

He *what*?

Love. How had that word escaped from the far recesses of his psyche? It wasn't even a word he used often. Was he *in love* with Zoe? Presumably, if a person was in love, they'd do everything in their power to shield their beloved from harm. To not only cherish but to protect. Logically, then, Jules himself was the potential harm to Zoe. Therefore, if he was in love with her, he should safeguard her from him. As a matter of fact, love obligated him to. Yes, he loved beautiful, sexy, talented Zoe Gaiman. So the most important thing he could do, the best way he could demonstrate his love, was to get out of her life.

His mission was clear.

When he'd left her earlier, inviting her to stay in the bath as long as she wanted and let herself out, they agreed to meet later at the apartment to supervise the furniture placement. At this point, perhaps it was going to be his father and a caretaker moving in, but nonetheless the renovation was coming to a close.

The front door was ajar when Jules arrived at the apartment, allowing him to see Zoe arranging some decorative items on the teakwood dining table that had arrived. The light streaming in through the windows added a golden halo to her natural radiance. His stomach clenched at the reminiscence of her satiny lips and of the responsive body that had arched for him over and over during their lovemaking. At the closeness that had formed without him being consciously aware of it, the secrets shared, the compassion for each other, the silly differences between them in the beginning so superficial now.

He'd allowed those forbidden daydreams he'd been having to crystalize into sharp focus for a split second. Them as a couple. His home as theirs. A kiss on the nose. Dancing by candlelight. Sharing an apple.

To have and to hold.

One last look at her through those rose-tinted glasses. Then he had to put a stop to his visions or they might kill him. In that respect, he *had* changed since childhood. Now he knew how to slay dragons, how to decimate obstacles that threatened him. Yes, that was it—love was an obstacle to freedom.

Zoe turned around as Jules entered the living room. "Oh. Hi. I didn't hear you come in."

"Did everything get delivered?"

"Si is doing a modification on the sofa sectional for me. Everything else came."

"Good."

"What's wrong?"

When Jules had abruptly raised himself out of the bathtub where they had been sharing a little slice of heaven a few hours ago, he hadn't explained about his mother's call from the Gare du Nord. While he'd shared quite a bit with Zoe about his past, he wasn't certain how much he should include her in any current matters. Now that he'd recognized what he needed to do, he was glad for that defensive decision.

Obviously, she was able to tell that something wasn't right. He moved nearer to her, though not too close, figuring it was better for him to say what needed to be said if he wasn't touching that honeyed skin he'd been caressing for hours last night after the opera.

"You know," he began, "we've never discussed any ongoing professional relationship after this project finished."

Zoe blinked a couple of times, sensing that the coming news was not good. "Ongoing professional relationship," she rasped the words he'd just spoken.

"I think you're a wonderful designer," he said, gesturing across the apartment. "It turns out all of your instincts were spot on after all, no matter how much I teased you about your methods."

"But..." She squinted.

Jules's lungs couldn't inhale a full breath. What he was about to say would alter the course of both of their lives forever. Compelled, but without the certainty he usually relied on for decisions, he carried on.

"What I'd like to do is connect you with some of the property developers I know here in Paris, who will hire you based on my recommendation. Smart and reliable designers are always in demand."

She nodded in comprehension, sweeping away some curls that had fallen forward. "So you're saying you wouldn't want to work with me again?"

Jules took a step forward but then forced his legs to stay put. Throwing his arms around her was the *wrong* thing to do in this moment. Yet, he couldn't stop fighting with himself about it.

"Zoe, I'm so sorry." *I love you.* "But I know myself well enough that I can't work with you again professionally because I can't see you anymore personally."

She jutted out her chin, choking back emotion. The entire set of her face changed, became drawn. "Oh, were we *seeing* each other?"

"Whatever it is we want to call it. To be perfectly honest, these weeks with you, making love, the Luxembourg Gardens, the opera, made me wonder for the first time in my life if I might be able to open up to a committed union with someone."

"And that someone isn't me."

"No." His Adam's apple pulsed. Frustration wasn't

allowing him to even say what he wanted to. "It is you. I've never felt anything for anyone like what I feel for you. That's the problem."

"I don't understand."

"I've never seen a healthy relationship in action. I wouldn't know what that looked like, how to do it. I'd ruin it. I'd never be capable of trusting someone or letting them put their trust in me. I'm better off as a ship that passes in the night."

"That's right, your three nautical voyages rule. I think with the opera we made it to four."

"You're angry. I'm so very sorry." *I love you.* "You've given me a taste of romance and enchantment. It was a divine state of being. But that's not for me, and never will be." He loathed rejecting her, the very person he'd most like to cherish until his dying day. Hated the words coming out of his mouth, even if they were the truth. For her and for him. His mind knew what his heart didn't want to accept.

Zoe composed herself. She was a survivor, too. He'd see to it that opportunities as a designer would come her way. He'd influence her future to the extent that he could from afar.

"We knew at the beginning that neither of us were intending to enter into anything serious," she stated bravely. "That was something we had in common."

After the loss of her parents, the risk of caring about someone and being cared for was great for her. She'd go it alone, too. Although her face said otherwise. Her eyes couldn't disguise the anguish.

With the weight of the world bearing down on him, Jules said, "I'll treasure this time together for the rest of my life."

Half of her mouth managed a hitch of a bittersweet smile. "Right. We'll always have Paris."

While she hadn't seen Jules enter the apartment a few minutes ago, Zoe surely watched him leave. As he walked out the door, the sight of the back of his head with the sharp swath of his dark thick hair and his slim frame in his pinstripe suit was unbearable in its perfection. She felt that her heart was attached to him and being stretched like a cord that would only go so far and then it would fray and disintegrate. Which it did when he disappeared out of view and she could finally let the tears flow.

After telling her that they'd no longer have a personal or professional relationship now that the work was done, he'd done a quick inspection of the completed apartment and then said he had another appointment. Zoe didn't know if that was true or that he just needed to get away from her. Which she could understand. He was clearly upset and conflicted—it wasn't as if he regarded calling things off with her lightly.

Her eyes couldn't turn away from the open front door as she wiped tear after tear from her eyes with the back of her hand. Even though she was in agreement with him that there was no future scenario that saw them together, the piece of her that had allowed visualizations of a different outcome stung and burned. It proved the point exactly, that Zoe didn't need any more pain, which would only have grown worse if the inevitable came after she'd become even more invested in Jules.

Once every fiber in her being was certain that he wasn't coming back to tell her, like he had at the opera, that he'd made another huge mistake, she pivoted in slow motion to take in the totality of the apartment. Without the strict budget that the clients she'd worked for back in Maupont were bound by, this apartment was Zoe's best career achievement so far. The practicality and accessibility, combined with the furnishings and appointments that announced style, had all come together whether Jules's parents would appreciate them or not.

She had the presence of mind to photograph the apartment for her portfolio. Jules had promised to act as liaison for her to get other design work in Paris, and for that she'd be forever grateful.

In the master bedroom, she'd talked Jules out of the rug he wanted because she was concerned that it was hard to maneuver over with the wheelchair. The bed was cool and inviting with baby blue and white linens. Twin nightstands held lamps and charging stations for electronics, with room for books or drinks. Gauzy curtains flanked the windows, and black-and-white seascape photographs adorned the sidewall. She'd had the wing-backed chairs returned to the shop she and Jules had bought them from, deciding instead on an upholstered bench from Si that would be easy for Hugo to use. There was plenty of passage space everywhere in the room.

Tears still streaming down her face, she snapped pictures of the second bedroom, which had been multipurposed nicely with a daybed that functioned as an extra sofa at an easy height for Hugo if he wanted it for afternoon naps or perhaps to enjoy the state-of-the-art television setup. Or if, in reality, the time came that he'd need a caretaker to spend the night. The long table underneath the picture window could be used for projects or as a desk, without the obstruction of drawers underneath.

The compromise about the kitchen that she and Jules had argued about worked perfectly, simple and clean cabinets painted off-white but with the yellow stone backsplash he'd wanted for a homey touch. Stacks of luxurious towels, storage shelves and artwork finished the bathroom. End tables place-marked where the sofa would fit into a corner in the living room, Jules having promised to send Zoe a photo when it came in.

Room by room, Zoe documented her accomplishments, exhaling loudly with no one to hear her, letting the tears continue to flow as they saw fit. When she was finished, she used the key codes to lock up, knowing this would be her last visit here. On the street, she walked toward the metro station, although not exactly sure of her destination. She didn't want to go home to an empty apartment, and Yasmine was at work at Si's studio.

Zoe descended the station stairs and decided where to go, though only halfway admitting it to herself. On the train, all the seats were taken so she grabbed onto one of the poles to anchor herself. From that position, she observed the fellow passengers surrounding her. That marvelous mix that was Paris, with people of every race, color, belief, orientation, size, age, homeland. Tourists, students, workers, families. Everybody headed somewhere. Stories to be told all around her.

Slitting her eyes to make her spying less obvious, she watched a young couple. The skinny man inked with tattoos up and down his arms held his dark-skinned gal from behind, pressing into her in a very sexual way, leaving no space between their bodies. She leaned her head back against his chest, a glazed-eyed bliss on her face. He whispered something into her ear that made her smile.

A city for lovers.

Zoe had been part of that folklore, ever so briefly. At the breathtaking loggia of the opera house. In the fine clothes and the diamond earrings Jules had bought her. Where her temporary lover kissed her without reserve and told her how much he wanted her in his bed again. How she'd floated up to the chandelier and Chagall ceiling after that, in an opaque trance for the rest of the performance while Jules maintained physical contact. At first, he'd held her hand, the pad of his thumb rhythmically caressing her skin. Later, he put his arm around her shoulder and held her there, the backs of his fingers stroking her neck.

In memory, what started on the loggia was one long embrace that lasted all night long, until they reveled in the morning's bubble bath. Zoe didn't know it at the time, but Jules's phone ringing signaled the alarm that would end the dream.

What would be the fate of the sexy couple Zoe eyed on the train? Happy forever or split by the weekend? Circumstances, wounds, fear, jealousy, fate, destiny. There were so many variables.

She exited at the station and trudged toward her destination. She entered the Luxembourg Gardens to wander around the perimeter of the café where she and Jules had been a pair of those Parisian lovers. Where they talked and laughed. Where she stuffed his face with a warm crepe and gooey pastries. She wouldn't have cared if they'd drunk plain water, as long as she was with him. The most amazing man she'd ever met.

A man of great intelligence and even greater character. Who awakened in her a primordial and grounded femininity that hadn't been unearthed before. Jules made her ping, made her second-guess her commitment to self-protection regardless of the cost. No one, nothing, would ever move her like he had. At least she hoped not.

When her phone rang as she wandered the gardens, she had a minute's hope that it was Jules until the screen identified a number she didn't recognize.

"Hello."

"Is this Zoe Gaiman?"

"Yes."

"This is Dr. Tran at Hospital Sainte-Térèse."

"Yes." Zoe's breath quickened. This couldn't be good.

"Yasmine Jaziri named you as her emergency contact."

"What happened?"

"Yasmine has been admitted into the hospital for observation. She collapsed at her workplace."

"I'll be right there."

CHAPTER NINE

ZOE COULD HEAR the clack of her own shoes as she rushed down the hospital corridor. She wasn't used to the sounds and the smells. Equipment in every direction blipped, dinged and beeped. There was an aroma of cleaning products that, no doubt, were responsible for the sterile whiteness of the hallways and floors.

"Yasmine Jaziri," she asked when she reached the nurses' station after following the instructions the doctor had given her over the phone. She'd left her session of disheartened reminiscing about Jules at the Luxembourg Gardens. As soon as she'd gotten the word about her roommate, she called for a rideshare, not wanting to spend time getting to the hospital on the metro.

Locating the room number the nurse gave her, Zoe poked her head in first, in case Yasmine was being attended to and needed privacy. Seeing that she was alone and asleep, Zoe tiptoed in so as not to wake her and sat down beside her bed in the visitor chair.

It was shocking to see Yasmine hooked up to tubes and wires. Some led to monitoring equipment. Zoe knew enough to note that her roommate's blood pressure and heart rate were stable, obviously a good sign. An intravenous line led to bags of fluids and medications. Yasmine seemed to be breathing normally while she slept. Although her dark complexion was more ashen than Zoe had ever seen it and her lips looked dry and chapped.

Time idled while she waited for Yasmine to wake up or for a doctor to enter with information. Zoe scanned everything in the room from an interior designer's point of view. It was drab but certainly functional, with a wall of built-in cabinets and drawers to organize supplies. Colorful geometric-patterned curtains tried to add some cheer as they flanked the one window. The view was of another building on the hospital's campus but it did allow in desperately needed natural light, as the overhead fixtures gave off a harsh illumination. Zoe thought she might go crazy from listening to the endless buzzing of equipment. Hospitals were not the most pleasant places.

"Well, hello there," Zoe said softly when Yasmine moved her head and slowly flickered open her eyes.

"Zoe," she scratched out, her throat obviously parched.

The bedside tray held a cup of water with a straw. "Are you allowed to drink anything?

"Yes, the nurse brought that before…before I fell asleep, I guess. My memory is a little fuzzy."

Zoe picked up the water and handed it to Yasmine, making sure the straw was close to her mouth and that she had a firm grasp on the cup.

"What happened?" The doctor on the phone said that Yasmine had collapsed but he hadn't had any further details.

After she took a few sips of the water, Yasmine handed the cup back to Zoe who returned it to the tray.

"One minute I was reaching for something on a high shelf and the next I was on the ground surrounded by the emergency medical responders Si had called for."

"Mademoiselle Jaziri, you lost consciousness," a low baritone joined the conversation as a man in a lab coat entered. "I am the attending physician, Dr. Tran."

He turned to Zoe. "You are a family member?"

"No, I'm Yasmine's roommate. Her family are all in Tunisia."

"Doctor…" Yasmine cleared her throat "…what is wrong with me?"

"It appears to have been severe dehydration. Everything looks okay but we'll need to do some more testing to see if there's an underlying condition and to make sure you didn't sustain any injuries when you fell."

"Oh, my gosh, what kind of injuries?"

"It's unlikely there are any based on the examinations and your present condition, but we'll want to do some brain imaging as a standard precaution."

Yasmine's eyes became wide as saucers. Zoe knew she was terrified and reached over to hold her hand. It was cold to the touch.

"I'll be back shortly and we'll get these assessments started as soon as we can. I really don't expect we'll find anything of concern, although we'll err on the side of caution."

"Thank you, Doctor," Yasmine managed as he left the room.

While the situation was serious, Zoe had long accepted that life was full of surprises. A young woman reaching up for something at work wasn't likely to crumple to the ground and need medical assistance. A hardworking couple going on a short holiday in Milan wasn't likely to be killed when a train ran off its track. Stuff happened.

Case in point, that in spite of the devastation Zoe had gone through after her parents' deaths that left her certain she'd never get close to anyone ever again, Jules Durand had happened. And it had shown her a prospect where two people did believe that they could be there for one another through thick and thin. Or were at least willing to give it a try and get by on hope.

Good fortune had actually graced Zoe. Jules called things off between them sooner rather than later. Any more days or nights she might have spent with him would have compounded the already heavy hurt she was towing like a ball and chain. Instead, at least now it was over and done. She didn't have to wait for the sneaky, inevitable stab to the chest. It had already come.

Alone she had decided to be. Alone she was. Everything was according to plan.

"That was a pretty good report from the doctor overall. How did you get so dehydrated, anyway? You did look a little bit off when I saw you at the studio."

"I got busy. I forgot to drink anything. Now that I think about it, it's been that way all week. I get involved in what I'm doing and I don't stop for breaks or lunch."

"That would never happen to me." Zoe smiled to cheer her up. "I eat all the time."

"With the hot billionaire?"

"Not anymore. That's old news."

"What? After the earrings? And the opera?"

Zoe touched one of the two diamonds that hadn't left her ears since Jules had placed them there. "My Parisian affair. That's all it was."

She'd known Yasmine for a year and while they co-existed peacefully as roommates, they weren't best friends. Zoe didn't have best friends. She was on her own in Paris, just as Yasmine was. Young women in a huge city, trying to forge a life for themselves but with no one watching their backs.

Yasmine's eyelids struggled to stay open.

"You should get some rest."

"Will you call my parents and tell them where I am? They're going to be so worried."

"I will."

Needless to say, Yasmine's mother was terribly distraught when Zoe explained the situation. With family and work obligations, neither of Yasmine's parents could immediately leave Tunisia for Paris to be by her side. Zoe promised to call her every time there was anything to report from the hospital. With audible tears, Yasmine's mother said that her daughter needed to move back to Bizerte, that this was the exact type of incident to prove that Paris was too far from home.

Zoe knew that a mother's love was talking rather than a voice of reason. But there was something to what she said, which directly related to the thoughts Zoe was starting to have. She sat back in the visitor's chair and propped her legs up on a corner of the bed while Yasmine slept. She was feeling rather tired herself.

Her fingers twisted one of the earrings. What Zoe had been mulling over was that maybe she should return home. To Maupont, to her siblings. Even though Jules had promised to act as liaison and find her more work, her brief time with him had only served to shed light on how lonely she really was. As much as she tried to outwardly present the idea that she didn't want or need anyone but herself, the lack of connections stared her in the face in this most social of cities. She no longer believed her own lies about choosing to go it by herself.

Boring Maupont. Designing the odd room renovation or workspace. But at least she'd have her brothers. They hadn't felt the ping in their chests, cautioning them not to get too close, not to feel. No warning alarm held them back. Two were married and she liked their wives. Perhaps they'd have children soon. That was something to look forward to. Fate might take any of them from her, but they'd have each other to rely on. She'd never be quite so solitary as she was now.

And as much as she loved Paris, she feared every building, every flower, every croissant would remind her of what she didn't get to have with Jules.

She leaned her head back and her eyelids grew heavy as, amidst the unfamiliar hospital drone, she allowed herself to drift off to sleep.

"I most certainly will not send you money. I've booked you a train ticket back to Paris yet again," Jules had scolded his mother, "and I expect you to use it."

With no options Agathe had, in fact, returned to the city. Jules had a driver pick her up at the train station and shuttle her to what was to be her new home. He and his father joined her there. Hugo greeted his wife with, "You again? I thought you promised never to return."

"This has got to stop!" Jules yelled. "Since you've been financially irresponsible for your entire lives and have no assets saved for your senior years, you are dependent on me. So you will live by my rules. Resent it or not, you've turned me into the parent. It should hardly be a horrible sacrifice to live in this apartment."

"Don't talk to us like we're children," Agathe tossed back with a snub of her nose.

"Yet, that's exactly how you behave."

"You wouldn't be the success you are if it weren't for us."

"You mean in spite of you."

"Don't talk that way to your mother," a gruff Hugo bellowed.

"Oh, have we found something you two agree on? That's a first." Jules frowned, finding himself unable to employ any self-censorship. This endless cycle with his parents was intolerable, and that wasn't all that was bothering him. "I introduced you to the interior designer who did the apartment. Both of Zoe's parents died in a train derailment."

Agathe blinked. "How awful."

"Yes, it's unimaginable. Life is fleeting. I can't understand why the two of you have chosen to live yours in constant opposition with each other."

"Your mother hates me because…"

"Enough excuses," Jules barked, cutting his father off. He'd had it and needed to fully express himself, to finally give voice to what he'd never said aloud to them. "Have either of you ever stopped to think what effect your constant fighting had on me, your only child? What it was like to have your mother leave with a suitcase over and over again, vowing never to return, even though she always did? And a father who couldn't keep a job because he was too stubborn to follow instructions and obey rules?"

A hush fell around them. His words were sinking in, both to himself and to them. It was liberating. To let out what he'd held inside. The words seemed to shock all three of them. After a lull, he found a calmer but pained voice, "Look at me. Really look at me. Beyond the professional success. Your son. Your child." He wanted to scream. For the boy who endured what he had. For the man who was crippled by the damage. "The atmosphere I grew up in of conflict, abandonment and uncertainty has left me unable to form relationships. I don't even have close friends. I've shut down any thoughts of marrying. Or having children. And I've only recently understood how much that has cost me."

Hugo and Agathe looked at each other, genuinely moved by their son's lament.

"I suppose we were too mired in our own strife to notice its impact on you," Hugo admitted.

Agathe shook her head as if she were just coming to a realization herself. "I was a horrible mother."

She was, and Jules was not going to assuage her with a denial. "What's done is done. But this has got to end. Because the craziest thing of it is that deep down you do care for each other. Why else would you, Mother, have always returned home when you left? And you, Father, always took her back? You could have split up. I'd hardly have been the first child whose parents had divorced. Yet, you didn't. And after I grew up, despite your bickering, you've roamed the world together."

"At your expense."

"That's not what matters. Life expectancies have gotten very long," Jules replied, "and even with father's physical limitations, you two could have several wonderful decades together. *We* could."

"What do you say, you nutty old bag?" Hugo threw a guffaw to his wife. "I suppose I must like you a little."

"All right, you good-for-nothing sod," Agathe answered back. "I might actually love you a little. No more drama."

"Let's not ask for the stars," Hugo snickered.

He wheeled his chair over to her and tugged on her arm until she leaned down for him to plant a kiss on her cheek.

Jules swallowed hard at the sight—he couldn't remember the last time he'd seen anything similar.

"You and Zoe did do a lovely job on this apartment," Agathe admitted.

"I know I've probably never said it, son," Hugo acknowledged, "but we're very proud of you." In fact, those weren't words he'd ever heard from his father. And for all of Jules's self-sufficiency, they meant a lot.

"Zoe and you?" Agathe inquired. "There's something between you that's more than just business, isn't there?"

How could his mother have intuited that during the short time they'd spent together at his hotel, when Agathe had been on particularly bad behavior? Was the bond between Jules and Zoe that obvious? Although it was almost impossible to say out loud words he didn't believe, he spat, "There was. There isn't anymore. How did you guess?"

"I can see it in your eyes. A mother knows." All three of them smirked at Agathe's comment as she was, obviously, anything but a typical mother. "I don't think you want to let her slip away."

After he left his parents to acquaint themselves with their new apartment, he got into the waiting car and picked up his phone. He remembered a school professor who'd said that one of the signs of a good leader was someone who would admit when they'd made a mistake. Jules had made the biggest one of his life. Even his mother could see it.

It was time to right the wrong. Witnessing his parents conceding to a reconciliation had moved him greatly. Gave him a new hope. Made him realize he was forever changed. He had a fresh distinction now. He was, and always would be, a man who had loved someone. Did love someone. And his mother was correct. The last thing he should do is turn his back on that precious gift of love. Yes, life came without guarantees. Yes, somebody with no experience in something was bound to stumble.

And yes, one could never be happy unless one followed his or her heart.

Jules's heart was walking around Paris on two curvaceous legs with a remarkable tangle of orange curls on its head. He needed to go claim that heart before it was gone and never to be found again.

When he tapped in the number to his heart's phone, the call switched directly to voice mail. What he had to say was too important to leave on a message. He did ask her to return his call as soon as possible. That it was urgent. He texted the same words and then instructed his driver where to take him.

Jules repeatedly rang the doorbell to Zoe's apartment. There was no response. He knew she wasn't at his parents' apartment, because he'd just left there. There was nothing else that needed to be purchased so she wasn't shopping for any finishing touches. Could she be out on a date? With a man, one who didn't put up barriers?

No, Jules assured himself. Zoe had been as adamant as he was that she would avoid the potential damage of love. He doubted she'd be out with a romantic interest so soon after he'd wounded her. She still might not be open to reconsidering her own rules. She'd been just like him in that respect. But the situation had changed. He'd have some convincing to do. That was okay. Whatever it took.

Not knowing what to do with himself, he went to a sports shop and bought two top-of-the-line bicycles for Zoe and Yasmine, and had them put in his car. He then had his driver return to Zoe's block. Perhaps she'd come home soon. He finished a sparkling water at a café before surrendering and going home. It wasn't until late that night when Zoe called and explained about Yasmine.

"Can I come to the hospital?"

"It's too late for visitors."

"Tomorrow, then."

"Let's wait and see."

Zoe woke up disoriented. Her phone buzzed in her pocket, but she let it go to voice mail. With eyes still closed, a backache reminded her that she'd been sleeping in a chair all night. She was still at the hospital. Although when her eyelids blinked open, she saw that neither Yasmine nor her bed were in the room with her. Zoe's mind whirled, imagining the worst, just as the hospital attendants wheeled Yasmine back into the room. She was sitting up in the bed and had a healthier color to her face.

"They took me downstairs for the brain imaging," Yasmine told Zoe. "I didn't want to wake you when I was wheeled out."

"Do we know anything?"

"No, but the doctor said he'll put a rush on getting the results. He thinks everything will be fine and that if I'm stable I can go home tomorrow."

Zoe stood to stretch. She felt like a twisted pretzel. And she was exhausted. While she'd managed to sleep here and there, she'd woken up many times during the night to the strangeness of the hospital. Darkness had finally opened into dawn. "If it's okay with you, I'm going to get some breakfast."

"You should. Thanks so much for staying with me."

"I'll be back in a little while."

Zoe forced her body into a fully upright posture and exited the room. Walking down the hospital corridor, she recalled the jumble of thoughts she'd had during the long night.

When her parents died, Zoe thought she'd never get over her grief. A black cloud blocked her from the sunlight for months after the accident. Their absence blinded her from seeing any goodness. The pain held her down, trying to strangle her.

That's when it all became certain. When she came to rely on the pings. In case she started to forget, the internal warning would remind her that she'd never let anyone close ever again. While two of her brothers went on to marry, and the other had a steady boyfriend, Zoe couldn't follow that path. Her heart was too soft. The risk was too high. In making her way to Paris, she'd vowed to throw herself into creativity and not people. She'd immunized herself like a vaccination would, preventing love from seeping into her bloodstream.

Over eggs and juice, Zoe was aware of the beeping in her pocket again. A glance at the phone screen told her not only that it was Jules but that she'd missed three of his calls. Why had he initially called yesterday? Something about the apartment, no doubt. Having briefed him last night about Yasmine, these morning calls were probably out of concern.

When she rang, he sounded relieved to hear the doctor's expected prognosis. "May I stop by?"

She didn't want him to come. Or did she? Jules wasn't part of Yasmine's life. He wasn't even part of hers anymore. He'd made a clean break with Zoe, and Yasmine's hospitalization didn't change that. She'd be better off continuing to practice being on her own, experiencing life's ups and downs such as roommates being in the hospital. "I don't think you should."

On the other hand, why wouldn't she want him to come? She didn't have many friends in Paris. Hospitals were big scary places. Why wouldn't someone want to have an ally, or even just a familiar face? How distorted her view of relationships had become. When she got back to Maupont, she'd put some genuine effort into finding a few girlfriends to pal around with, maybe university mates she'd lost touch with.

Solitude suddenly washed over her like an ocean's wave.

Jules said, "I'd like to see the both of you."

Zoe had a moment to protest. She didn't take it.

Zoe was back in Yasmine's room when Jules stepped into the doorway. A sight for sore eyes to be sure, he held a beautiful arrangement of yellow flowers in a glass vase. "May I come in?"

"Of course," Yasmine answered, shooting a knowing look in Zoe's direction.

"These are for you." He placed the flowers down on the stand beside Yasmine's bed.

"They're so pretty. Thank you."

They conversed a bit until Yasmine's eyelids began to flutter. Jules took the cue. He stood at her bedside. "Assuming you're going home tomorrow, can I give you a ride?" He knew that Zoe and Yasmine were alone in Paris, with no family, and he thought of a way he could be useful. That was one of the many things Zoe lo...

"That would be wonderful. Thank you," Yasmine said as her eyes fell shut.

"Step into the hallway for a minute with me?" he asked Zoe, who was on the other side of the bed. She nodded, although apprehension bounced in her stomach.

"What were you calling about last night?" Zoe wasted no time once they'd left the room. To be with Jules in the antiseptic surroundings of the hospital was unnatural. Wrong. And it almost angered her. This was a place for families, for significant others, for lifelong relationships. Where people died or were healed or brought babies into the world. It wasn't a place for Parisian bosses and the underlings they'd had affairs with to chat.

He made contact with her pupils and followed them when they tried to move away. "Do you remember when we went to the opera and I told you I wanted a do-over?"

"Yes."

"I need an even bigger one this time. I've made another horrible error. And I'm here to correct it." He wrapped his hand around her small shoulder, his warmth instantly radiating through his palm into her. "I want to be with you, Zoe. I don't know what I'm doing and I'm bound to take dozens of wrong turns but I love you. And we're going to be together."

Overwhelm had her feeling dizzy. She'd spent the wee hours of the night making sense of his breakup, re-affirming her aloneness. He'd been crystal clear, know-ing himself, stating his mind. Now he'd changed it and she was just supposed to jump in? Her internal ping sig-naled so loud and fast she was sure the nurses in another ward were going to confuse it with medical equipment.

"I can't, Jules. You helped me realize that. I'm not good for anyone."

"You're good for me! Just when I was sure I'd be alone forever, something I wouldn't have predicted in a million years occurred. You. You fell, literally, into my life," he teased her about her first impression, "and you destroyed my ordered world with its rule books and protocols. You've shown me that our hearts can be free. And limitless."

When he'd told her at the apartment that he didn't want to see her anymore professionally or personally, that was news she hadn't thought she could move past. Instead, it was this, the opposite, that was even harder. To turn away from what half of her admitted she so desperately wanted. Yet, she had to. She was the only one there to protect her. Zoe had to be her own knight in shining armor.

"I'm sorry. I can't."

After they stood in the corridor staring silently at each other for as long as they could take, Zoe granted Jules's request to return to the hospital the next day to take Yasmine home. She couldn't deny him that.

"Tomorrow, then."

Time passed with Yasmine undergoing many exams

and tests, and the two roommates making the best of hospital television programming. The nurses were kind enough to give Zoe soap and towels so that she could shower, as she didn't want to go home and leave Yasmine alone at the hospital.

During the artificially lit hours of the night, Yasmine slept peacefully while Zoe's mind whirled. Even though she might have wished for Jules's return, she hadn't been expecting it. Forcing her to face her demons yet again, to reconsider what was real and what she was hanging onto simply because it had become familiar. After endless cups of tea from the kind nurses, and after running down her phone's battery wasting time on the internet looking at furniture, Zoe decided to take a little walk around the hospital ward.

She was used to the blinking lights and identifying sounds by now. There was very little other noises beside a faint and constant buzz. Visiting hours were long since over. A custodian mopped the floor. Someone else restocked bedding onto a cart. Zoe didn't mean to snoop but she glanced into a couple of patients' rooms as she passed them by. A very elderly man, tiny and frail, breathed with the help of an oxygen mask on his face. In the next, a much younger man had bandages on his head. Had he undergone surgery, she wondered? Or had he fallen? Had he been in an accident? Was he the victim of a crime? Her brow furrowed in concern. He couldn't have been much older than twenty.

How unknowable the universe was! Look what had happened even just in her orbit. Yasmine's spell of dehydration could have made her collapse while crossing a street, where she might have been hit by a car, or could have broken her legs or sustained brain damage that left her unable to walk or talk. Zoe's parents might have traveled safely to Milan and be home in Maupont right now. Every moment of existence was a treasurable gift that needed to be treated as such and never taken for granted.

And Zoe finally couldn't deny that however many days and nights she had left on this earth, she wanted more than anything to spend them with Jules. With him, the world could be complete and full and she could belong. She knew that she'd helped him find a little whimsy and delight from within the seriousness of his life, the fallout of his past. But he probably didn't know how much he'd given her, besides just a job.

Without intending to, he made her feel connected to him and part of something larger than herself, something that mattered and was worth having at any cost. Together, they were an interdependent entity. He taught her that planning for the future wasn't to be feared, that it could be a positive thing. His commitment to his parents in spite of what they put him through moved her. In his arms, she'd learned about a joining of souls and bodies far beyond what she'd ever known was possible. And she wanted to keep experiencing that merge for eternity. They sometimes had opposite ways of looking at things but like yin and yang, Jules and Zoe fit together as a whole.

She would never get over the grief of her parents' untimely deaths. Nor should she. Grief was a measure of her love for them. The grief could be welcomed. It could be cherished. And most importantly, Zoe needed to stop using it as an obstacle.

She was in love with Jules Durand. And she needed

to tell him so as soon as possible. Hopefully, it wasn't too late.

Dawn couldn't come fast enough.

With morning cheer, she phoned to let Jules know that Yasmine was being discharged. "Everything is okay. She can go home."

"That's wonderful. I'll be right there."

After he arrived and while Yasmine was collecting her personal belongings to leave, Zoe took Jules's hand to pull him aside. The smile that lit up his eyes told her that nothing had been jeopardized, nothing would ever be too late. She caressed the back of his hand with her thumb. "This time it's me who needs a do-over."

He began nodding excitedly. "Yes. Yes, my love. I think we've got a lot to work through between us. We're going to make many mistakes. Need many do-overs."

"We'll get through them."

"Does Yasmine take good care of herself as a rule? Does she eat plenty of vegetables and take vitamins?"

"I think so. Nice of you to inquire." Zoe's health-conscious man. Was her future going to include icky green drinks and early morning runs? That was okay if that's what he wanted. As long as there were pajama days and plenty of cheese, too. She'd hope to live a long and balanced life. With Jules.

"I'm asking because I want to make sure she'll be okay on her own."

"What do you mean?"

"I was thinking that perhaps she could move into one of my properties."

"Why? Where will I live?"

"I want you to move in with me. And marry me. And be by my side for the rest of our days. Will you do that?"

"I will." The cautioning ping in her gut almost tore her open. That was another thing she'd have to walk with, to accept. She could do it. As long as she was with him. "I love you, too, and I want to be with you forever." Zoe threw her arms around Jules with a force that knocked even him off-kilter. Something she was very good at.

* * * * *

LET'S TALK
Romance

For exclusive extracts, competitions
and special offers, find us online:

f facebook.com/millsandboon

⬤ @millsandboonuk

🐦 @millsandboon

Or get in touch on 0844 844 1351*

For all the latest titles coming soon,
visit millsandboon.co.uk/nextmonth

Want even more
ROMANCE?

Join our bookclub today!

'Mills & Boon books, the perfect way to escape for an hour or so.'

Miss W. Dyer

'Excellent service, promptly delivered and very good subscription choices.'

Miss A. Pearson

'You get fantastic special offers and the chance to get books before they hit the shops'

Mrs V. Hall

**Visit millsandbook.co.uk/Bookclub
and save on brand new books.**

MILLS & BOON